ALDERI
- Book One -

SECRETS

A Fantasy Adventure

RICHARD BOWEN

Copyright © 2020 Richard Bowen

All rights reserved, including the right to reproduce this book, or portions thereof in any form. No part of this text may be reproduced, transmitted, downloaded, decompiled, reverse engineered, or stored, in any form or introduced into any information storage and retrieval system, in any form or by any means, whether electronic or mechanical without the express written permission of the author.

This book is a work of fiction. Although the physical setting of the book is the Island of Alderney in the Channel Islands and all place names are factual, the names, characters and incidents are either products of the authors' imagination or are used fictitiously. Any resemblance to actual events or persons, living or dead, is entirely coincidental.

The views expressed in this work are solely those of the author and do not necessarily reflect the views of the publisher, and the publisher hereby disclaims any responsibility for them.

ISBN: 978-0-244-27582-2

PublishNation
www.publishnation.co.uk

Dedicated to my grandchildren

Preface

The island of Alderney is the most northerly of the Channel Islands sitting just 7 miles off the coast of North West France. Approximately 3 miles long and with a population of barely 2000, the magical island of Alderney holds many secrets. Victorian forts, German World War II fortifications, a Roman fort, tunnels, caves, and many other mysteries and wonders.

A crime-free paradise that gives children and families a safe haven to explore and enjoy life to the full. Where children are able to grow up safely and, more importantly, explore and play to their heart's content without adults interfering!

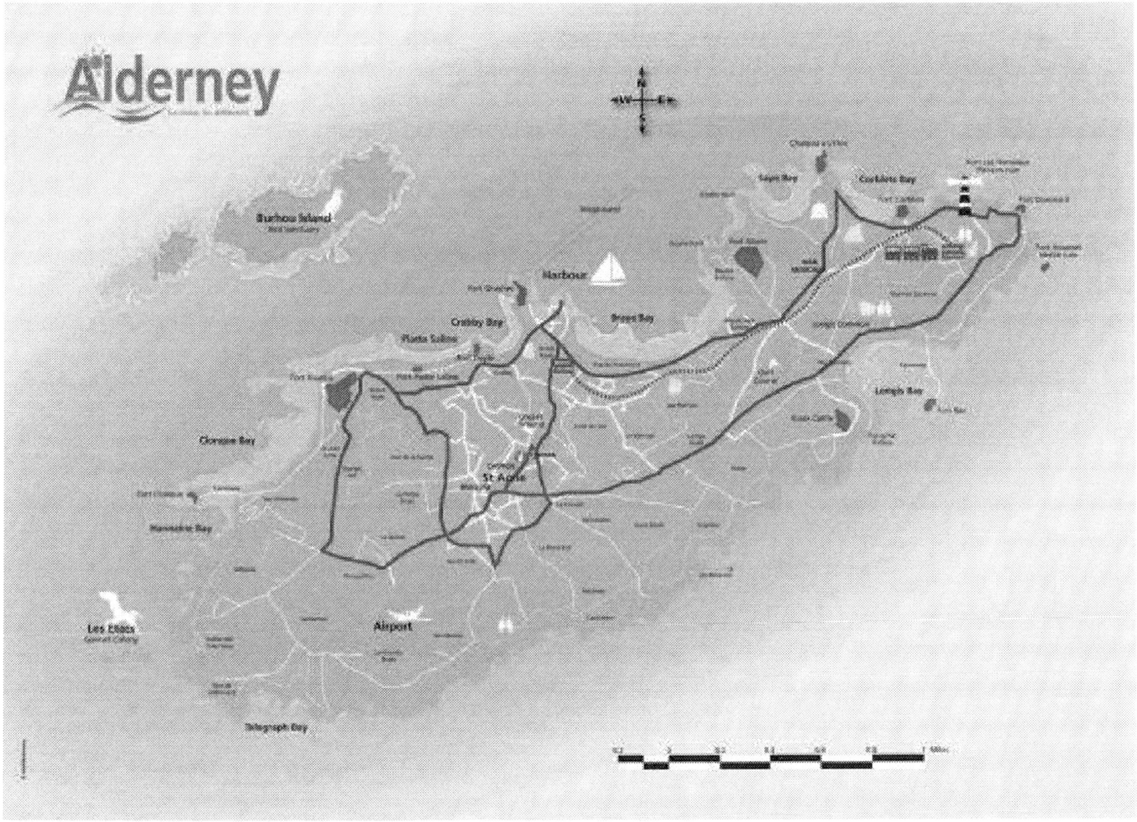
Alderney
N
W
E
S
Burhou Island
Harbour
Saye Bay
Corblets Bay
Braye Bay
Crabby Bay
Platte Saline
Clonque Bay
St Anne
Longis Bay
Hannaine Bay
Les Etacs
Airport
Telegraph Bay
1 Miles

CHAPTER 1

"Hurry up!" Alex bellowed as he threw a pebble up to Ben's bedroom window. "We'll be late."

It was 5.30 in the morning and Alex was in a hurry. They were supposed to be meeting up with Luis and Chloe that morning down at the harbour.

As the sun slowly came into view over Fort Albert to the east, the reflection from his watch dazzled Alex. *I've been stood here ten minutes already,* he thought. One last try to wake Ben.

He sauntered over to where he'd parked his Vespa 50cc scooter and opened his backpack. Alex had packed the backpack the night before with his usual assortment of odds and ends. Torch, mobile phone, a reel of fishing line he'd borrowed from his Dad, a tin box with lead weights and hooks inside and a length of rope. A pack of sandwiches were screwed up in the corner of the bag with a can of juice and a couple of apples.

Just as he was about to give up looking, he spotted his woollen hat. Concealed inside was a golf ball. *That'll do,* he thought.

Alex walked back to beneath Ben's bedroom window and with one swing of his arm the golf ball flew upwards and unerringly hit the glass window, shattering into a thousand pieces. *Oops,* Alex thought, as he raised his hand to his mouth in an attempt to stop himself laughing.

Alex turned away as he struggled to stop himself from laughing when he felt a thump on the back of his head. "Ouch" he screamed as he realised what had happened. Looking back up to what was left of the window pane he could see Ben leaning out with a big grin on his face.

"Serves you right" Ben shouted. "Look at the mess you've made".

Alex sighed as he picked up the golf ball and placed it back in the backpack on his scooter. *That really hurt* he thought as he grimaced once more.

"I'll be down in a mo" Ben shouted.

Alex hadn't heard Ben as in that moment he was deep in his own thoughts. *That was stupid. I've now got a pane of glass to pay for and I've only got my money that I've saved from selling golf balls.*

Alex lived near the challenging island 9 hole golf course and he would spend most evenings on the course looking for golf balls that had been lost with wayward shots from the local players. Each morning he would place a box full of golf balls at the end of the drive to the house with a sign, GOLF BALLS FOR SALE £1 EACH. Passers by would always buy them ...

"Alex! ALEX!!"

Alexs' thoughts were interrupted by the shouts from Ben who by now had crept up behind Alex to surprise him.

Alex turned round to realise his friend was stood right next to him. "Sorry about the glass, I'll pay for it" Alex said as he looked down to Ben as he was considerably shorter than him.

"To right you will" Ben exclaimed and then with that grin of his "Nah, forget it, I'll tell my Mum it was a bad shot by a golfer!"

They both laughed.

As they both laughed the recognisable sound of a 50cc Honda scooter was drawing closer. They both knew it was a Honda as a 4 stroke engine had a deeper, richer sound than the 2 stroke engine of Alexs' Vespa. Most teenagers who lived on

Alderney could ride a scooter. Something that wasn't possible in most countries.

The boys knew who it would be this early in the morning. The noise from the Honda grew louder until a screech of brakes signalled the approaching scooter had hit the nearby bend close to Bens' house. "That'll be the girls then!" said the boys in union and they laughed.

"Yeah, Lillys' steering doesn't get any better" Ben joked.

Alex was still nodding in agreement as the Honda screeched to a halt as it mounted the pavement.

The engine spluttered to a halt and as the two girls jumped off, both boys shouted "Hi Lilly. Who's this you've got with you?"

They knew it was Usha, Lillys' sister. They loved to wind her up because Usha had a very short fuse and lost her temper very quickly, but in a funny sort of way. Usha pulled off her crash helmet, her shoulder length curly blonde hair glinting in the early morning sunlight. Even though she was only 15 years old Usha was independent and her confidence outweighed her young age. She strutted every inch of her 54 inch height up to Ben and pushed him over.

"You know who I am" Usha yelled as she stood over Ben.

"Usha" Lilly shouted in a certain dominating tone, "That's enough".

"Or what?" Usha boomed.

"Just cut it out" Lilly demanded. "Say sorry to Ben and forget it".

At that, Usha grabbed hold of Bens hand and pulled him to his feet. "Sorry Ben" Usha said with an impish grin.

"Good to see you both" Alex said with a smile. "Got everything you need?" he asked Lilly.

"Of course we have" she retorted. She was a confident 16 year old. Clever, attractive, quite slim with long straight blonde hair who always caught the boys' eyes at the local school. Lilly was the tallest of this group of friends and so it seemed on most occasions, she was the natural leader.

"Come on you lot, let's get going" Lilly said as she scanned the small group with her piercing blue eyes. "The other two will be wondering where we are", and at that the four of them scooped up their backpacks and scrambled up and onto their scooters.

Luis and Chloe were sat on the diners' tables outside the local chip shop come restaurant which looked out over the small but busy inner harbour.

"I wonder where the others have got too" Chloe asked as she punched Luis in the side of his ribs.

"Dunno" Luis grunted as he winced from Chloes' playful punch. "I suppose they've had to wait for Ben as usual. He's such a lazy sod don't you think?" and with that, Luis continued to peer through his binoculars at the horizon looking to see how many container ships were passing by in the distance on their way up through the English Channel.

Chloe gazed at Luis' torso in admiration. He was the new kid on the island and was a bit of a hunk. Thick black shaggy hair that fell to his well muscled shoulders. His semi bronzed skin was just crying out to be caressed. He was a good athlete. She'd watched him at school running on the track and playing football. In the few weeks he had been on Alderney, Luis had made quite an impression with the girls. *If only I could make him see ...* and in that moment, the sound of scooters approaching interrupted Chloes' thoughts.

Luis jumped down from the table, passing his binoculars to Chloe. "About time" he mumbled as the scooters roared into view.

Lilly and Alex gave each other a knowing glance and yelled "Hang on" as they pulled the handlebars towards them causing the front wheels to lift from the ground. Ben and Usher clung on with all their strength as the scooters wheelied across the road and came to a shuddering halt a few yards in front of Luis and Chloe.

"I suppose you think you're clever" Chloe shouted.

Luis just stood his ground, opened mouthed. He felt a playful punch to his stomach, not for the first time that morning, as Chloe shouted at him "What are you gawping at?". Luis was lost for words for once. His warm dark brown eyes were transfixed as he gazed unashamedly at Lilly. "Helloooo" Chloe yelled right in front of Luis' face. "Get a grip boy" she growled and then punched him again.

Ben, Alex and Lilly jumped off the scooters and ran over to Chloe and Luis where they were stood hands on hips. A look of panic appeared on their faces.

"What's up Chloe?" Alex asked.

She didn't say anything but just pointed towards the two scooters. They all turned to see Usha lying motionless on the ground pinned down by a scooter that had tipped over on its side. They all immediately started to move towards where Usha was lying.

"Stay back" Lilly shouted as they got closer.

"But …" and before Ben could finish,

"No, stay away …. please, I know what I'm doing" Lilly insisted. "Just keep away".

Lilly knelt down hiding Usha from view of the others. Lilly turned her head towards the others, "Usha's fine, just give us a minute", as she gestured to the others to stay back.

Turning back to Usha, Lilly then held Ushas' head with her left hand. She could see that her left leg was broken in two places and blood was pouring out of a dip gash on her left arm onto the road surfacing. "Usha" Lilly whispered, "Grab my amulet".

Usha reached out to touch the amulet around Lillys' right wrist and as she did so the amulet released an intense yellow halo and in an instant it was gone. All signs of the injuries had disappeared, Usha was healed.

"Usha, you can get up now" Lilly whispered. "If the others say anything just tell them you was pretending to be hurt to give them a scare. And give them that grin of yours, it always works."

The two girls jumped up from the ground and quickly joined the others.

"What?" Usha said to the group that had by now surrounded her. "That got you all going eh" Usha said and her face contorted with that huge impish grin of hers.

Ben and Alex playfully pushed her as they all burst into laughter.

"Typical Usha" Chloe said, "Always the joker".

Luis stood there silently, quite dumbfounded at what he'd just witnessed.

"Come on" Lilly shouted, "Enough mucking about, let's get going".

This Saturday had been planned a couple of days before. Meet up at the chippy before heading off to the north west of the island to explore Fort Tourgis before spending the night there in tents.

The group climbed up onto their scooters. Chloe upfront with Luis sat behind, Alex with Ben and Lilly with Usha.

"You take the lead Chloe" Lilly shouted. "Go on Alex, you follow them. I'll catch you all up in a mo" and at that the two scooters roared off.

"You okay?" Lilly enquired as she turned to look at Usha.

"Yeah, fine" Usha replied, "Just hurry up and text Grandad to let him know. We need to catch the guys up before they start to wonder or have suspicions".

Text …
Hi Grandad. Need to get
To Chippy. Burn mark.
Thanks. Lilly x

"Okay, done" Lilly said, "Hold on sis, don't want you falling off, ha!" The scooter started first time and away they went in hot pursuit of the others.

CHAPTER 2

Buzz buzz, buzz buzz, bu…. Richards' hand hit his mobile phone to stop the noise as he rolled over in bed. He peered through half opened eyes, "Jeez, who's this at half past six in the morning?"

Richard pressed a button to open the text on his phone. *Here we go again* he thought to himself, *it's Lilly*, and as he read he clambered out of bed, still half asleep. "Right, better get cracking and go and clean up any potential trouble" he grumbled.

Twenty minutes later and Richard climbs into his old shop van. He'd owned and run a convenience store on the island for over twelve years and he'd not long retired. After a couple of goes with the ignition key, the engine spluttered into life. *Must get this van serviced sooner rather than later* he thought. After a couple of revs, it was into gear and on his way.

It was a five minute drive down to the chippy. That's about the average drive time in Alderney, nothing is very far away. *The van seemed a bit sluggish this morning* Richard thought. *Just as well on this little lane down the hill with all these loose chickens strutting around looking for scraps of food.* A nearby friend kept about sixty chickens in the field running parallel to the lane. Trouble is, chickens don't stay in fields, especially when there are no fences!

As Richard scanned the field to the left there was the usual commotion of chickens running around aimlessly chased by the odd cockerel. He could see a couple of chickens entering one of the assorted sized hen houses dotted around the field. *Egg laying time* thought Richard.

To the back of the field stood an old stable which was the overnight shelter for the two horses which also occupied the field. They were slowly munching on the vegetation underneath one of the three wind scorched hawthorn trees. Over the years the trees had grown at an angle from west to east due to the strong winter westerly winds giving the appearance of lopsided umbrellas.

Richards' gaze turned back to the lane in front of him. "Whooaa!" he shouted, as he swerved to avoid hitting the last remaining chicken in the road. "Stupid bird" he shouted to himself, if only to compose himself.

Richard slowed as he reached the junction with the road from the right at Ladysmith bend. The bend in the road formed a sort of bridge over a stream that came from a spring further up the hill. The stream ran into a water trough below the bridge before overflowing through the lush vegetation into the valley below. Walkers and the like would often follow the footpath around Ladysmith.

Strange name Richard thought. He'd often wondered about it.

Richard stepped on the accelerator and the van coasted further down the hill passing a footpath to Fort Tourgis on his left. The sea and the horizon was now in view directly ahead. The smell of seaweed was in the air and the crashing of waves could be heard.

The van slowed as Richard drove up to the junction with the main coastal road. To his left was the old water mill which was currently being restored to its' former fully working glory. Further over to the left on Tourgis Hill was the huge Victorian structure, Fort Tourgis.

Richard turned right onto the main road, Platte Saline. A couple of digger drivers were already working on the beach to his left. Platte Saline beach is a long stretch of predominately gravel chippings which the local builders use during their working day.

The sun was really bright today thought Richard as he adjusted the visor to stem the glare away from his eyes. To his right were an assortment of bungalows which were set back from the road. Long drives giving the impression of self importance for the occupiers.

One particular property always stood out for Richard. The building was nothing special but the significance of its' history was important. *Sad*, Richard thought as he drove past.

The two huge pillars either side of the entrance to one of the concrete driveways on his right marked what remained of part of Alderneys' dark past harking back to the second world war. There are many other examples across the island. These pillars are poignant in the fact that they indicate the entrance to what was a prisoner of war camp during that dark episode of history. *Really sad*, Richard thought.

Richard sped on, and up onto the road travelling around Crabby bay, another stony beach with Fort Doyle, which was built in 1793, on the left and the local state of the art hospital up to the right.

The chippy was in sight. Richard slowed the van as he looked around to make sure the coast was clear. He didn't need any awkward questions this morning.

Richard pulled up outside the chippy. He'd spotted the position where Lilly had used her amulet. It always left a scorched mark about the size and shape of a rugby ball. He manoeuvred the van into position so that the front wheel was next to the mark.

Right, let's get this sorted, Richard thought as he jumped out of the van. He slid open the side door and pulled out a spare wheel and propped it up against the front wheel of the van. He pulled his left sleeve of his shirt up his arm to reveal an amulet identical to Lillys'. It consisted of 12 different coloured crystals. Richard placed his hand on the scorched mark and in that moment the amulet released an intense red halo. The scorched mark had gone.

"Hello", a shout in the distance.

"Hello".

The shout was closer. Richard turned to see a fisherman coming towards him from the harbour. Richard knew him. It was Alexs' father.

"Oh hi Frank. How you doing?" Richard enquired trying to stay calm. He could feel his hands shaking as he pulled his shirt sleeve back down to hide the amulet.

"You alright Richard?" Frank asked.

"Yeah, I'm good thanks" Richard replied trying to keep his voice steady.

"It's just that I thought"

"Thought what Frank?" Richard interrupted him.

Frank had that enquiring look on his face "It's probably nothing, but I thought I saw a strong flash of red light up here".

"Probably the sun reflecting off something Frank. Maybe a piece of glass" Richard responded. "Nothing to worry about I wouldn't think eh Frank?"

"Nah, suppose you could be right Richard. Anyway, what are you doing here this early in the morning?" Frank asked.

"Changing this wheel" Richard replied as he grabbed the spare wheel. "I'd just finished when I heard you shout" and with that, Richard stood up and through the wheel in the van and slid the door closed with a thud.

"So Frank, you been out in the bay putting your lobster pots out?" Richard asked.

"Yeah, right" Frank muttered. "Actually, I meant to say, I spotted your grand daughter Lilly and some friends including my lad Alex early this morning on their scooters. Looked like they were on their way up to Fort Tourgis".

"Oh right" Richard replied with a smile.

"Those scooters are death traps Richard. You need to have a word with Lilly and her friends" Frank said.

"Yeah, I will do Frank" Richard retorted. "Thanks for the concern. I'll see you around. Got to go now". Richard jumped in the van and turned the ignition. The engine spluttered into life and with a full turn of the steering wheel the van spun round. Richard heaved a sigh of relief and thought to himself, *text Lilly and then get myself some breakfast.*

"Come on van, need to get home" Richard shouted to himself as he watched Frank disappear into the distance in his rear view mirror.

CHAPTER 3

Lilly and Usha skidded to a halt on the gravelled parking area just before the turnoff at the bottom of Tourgis Hill.

Across the road at the base of the hill is another reminder of the second world war fortifications you find on Alderney. A huge concrete bunker which would have been built around 1942. It would have housed anti tank guns to defend the beach and bay from invaders.

"Just checking my phone Usha before we reach the others".

"Okay, hurry up" Usha replied.

"Right, Grandad's cleaned up. Let's go" Lilly said.

"Hang on sis". With a twist of her wrist the scooter shot forward and turned onto the narrow coastal lane which led to

Fort Clonque about half a mile away on the other side of the bay.

As Lilly steered the scooter along the lane Usha gazed up to her left admiring the vast scale of the Victorian stonework of Fort Tourgis. The lane veered around to the left and took them to the small car park where their friends scooters were parked.

"Where are they?" Usha asked.

"Not sure" Lilly replied. "They can't be far away."

"Alex, Ben" Lilly shouted.

"Hello" Usha yelled. "Is anyone around?"

"Over here" a voice boomed from behind where the girls stood.

"In here" another voice from behind them sounded.

"That's Chloes' voice" Lilly said.

The two girls turned to see an old wooden door open just to the right of a wooden bench at the rear of the parking area. The door was partly hidden by a tangled mess of brambles and ivy which cascaded down the western stone walls and banks of Fort Tourgis.

"Come on Lilly, let's see what the others are up to" Usha said.

The girls picked up their backpacks and walked over to the partly opened wooden door. The door creaked as Lilly grabbed hold of it. Usha stepped inside with Lillys' hand on her shoulder.

"Careful Usha, watch your step, it's quite dark in here" Lilly said.

The girls stood still letting their eyes adjust to the semi darkness.

"We're over here" Ben shouted.

Lilly could just make out the silhouetted shape of Ben towards the back of the space in front of her. A bright beam of light suddenly shone into their eyes temporarily blinding them.

"Sorry girls" Ben shouted as he lowered his torch to light up the floor in front of Lilly and Usha. "Walk towards the main light".

The girls could now see that the floor was covered in thick dust that had obviously built up over many years. All manner of tools and rubbish were scattered across the floor.

"Be careful where you walk girls" Ben said "All sorts of stuff all over the place".

The girls gingerly walked across the floor brushing away cobwebs that were in front of them with their hands until they reached Ben.

"We need a light in here" Usha grumbled.

"Yeah I know" Ben replied. "This place hasn't been used in years and there doesn't seem to be any power. There's a light bulb hanging down from the roof above your heads but it doesn't work. The others are further back in here looking to see if they can find a light bulb that works" and Ben turned to point his torch to highlight the others.

In an instant, Lilly reached up to the light fitting. The amulet spontaneously emitted a white halo and disappeared in a flash, leaving the hanging light bulb above them shining brightly.

Ben spun round. "What?" Ben exclaimed.

"I just touched it" Lilly said, "Must have been a bad connection" and she smiled at Usha.

The three others stopped looking amongst the assorted items in front of them and joined Lilly, Usha and Ben.

"Good work Lilly" Chloe said, "Certainly better with some light in this place.

"So Ben, what is this place?" Alex asked with an enquiring look on his face.

"Yeah, come on Ben, what is it?" added Luis.

"It's an old German second world war ammunition store" Ben explained. "My dad was given the use of it by a local carpenter a couple of years ago just before the guy died. He also used to renovate old furniture and he was really interested with antiques, especially jewellery and the like".

Lilly gave Usha a knowing glance.

Ben continued. "The trouble is, this place is too far out of the way for my Dad to use it as a workshop so he hasn't done anything with it. Shame really, but he won't give it to anyone else 'cos this carpenter guy was a big friend of his. So there you go. I think my Dad's been in here once to store some tents away".

"Yeah, I know the guy was a big friend of my Grandad" Lilly chimed in "a really good guy, a sad day when he died". At that point Lilly could feel tears welling up in her eyes and she turned away momentarily to compose herself. Usha held Lillys' hand reassuringly. She knew how Lilly felt.

"So what are we doing here?" Lilly asked.

"Well" Ben said, "Somewhere in here are a couple of tents that my Dad put in here a couple of years ago. I thought we could use them up in the grounds of Fort Tourgis. The weather's looking good overnight so I thought it would be cool to camp out tonight. What do you think?"

"Yeah, come on Lilly. Should be good" Luis said with the others nodding in agreement.

"Right then, sounds like a good idea" Lilly said. "We'd better crack on and find these tents. We'll need some sleeping bags as well".

"No probs" Ben replied, "My Dad reckons there should be about ten in here".

Chloe and Usha looked at Ben with quizzical looks.

"When the lease at the camp site over at Saye Bay changed hands, I think about six years ago, they sold everything off cheap and bought a load of new stuff to kit the camp site out with more modern gear" Ben explained.

"So there could be other bits and pieces in here we could use if we're camping tonight? Alex asked.

"Yeah, sure" Ben replied.
"Right, let's get looking" Usha said.
"Found the tents" Luis shouted.
They all cheered "Hurrah".

As the others continued to rummage around the chaotic mess, Lilly took the opportunity to carefully scan the area looking for anything that could possibly explain why she felt connected in some way to this place. She was sure it had something to do with her Grandad and his friend that had died. Lilly just couldn't put her finger on it. *Gonna have to chat to Grandad about this place*, Lilly thought.

A shout from Chloe cut through Lillys' thoughts. "Found the sleeping bags guys and luckily I've just found a mallet. Be handy for knocking in the tent pegs".

"Cool" Ben said. "Let's get this gear outside and then we can park the scooters in here for the night. They'll be safe in here".

The group picked up the tents and sleeping bags and dumped them on the gravel in the car park.

"Right, let's get the scooters inside" Ben ordered.

Alex grabbed hold of his scooter and wheeled it through the door, followed by Chloe and then Lilly.

As they turned and reached the door to head back outside Lilly said "I'll turn the light off". Standing behind the door out of sight she placed her left hand on her forehead and raised her right hand to reveal the amulet. In an instant, a white halo emitted from the light bulb and seemed to be absorbed by the amulet. Darkness once more.

As Lilly stepped outside into the bright sunlight, Ben grabbed hold of the creaking wooden door and pulled it shut. He then locked it and put the old key in his jacket pocket. "You found a light switch Lilly?" Ben asked.

"Yes" Lilly replied.

CHAPTER 4

It had been a long haul up the hill with their backpacks, tents and sleeping bags and as they approached the huge stone built arch which was the main entrance to Fort Tourgis at the end of the grass track the group had been following they all stopped to read the rusting metal sign high up on the wall to the left.

Luis read out loud, "Danger, this building is unsafe. Enter at your own risk".

"Take no notice Luis" Chloe said, "Loads of visitors come up here to look around. You've just got to be careful".

"Yeah Luis" Ben added, "And that goes for all of us" as he gave all of them a look. "Some parts of the fort are really unsafe, so yeah, we have to be careful. Got it?"

The group all nodded as they walked through the arch. In front of them was a flattish grassed area the size of half a football pitch. To the left were stone walls with ramparts probably fifteen metres in height. On the right stood the main structure about twenty metres high with a low stone wall running the entire length in front. And so it went on. Everywhere the group looked, it was Victorian history.

"Awesome" Usha exclaimed.

"Right" Lilly said, "We need to find somewhere suitable for these tents.

"What's wrong with this flat area here?" Luis asked.

"It's all stonework underneath this grass" Lilly explained, "It was probably some sort of parade ground for the soldiers back in the day, or maybe a communal courtyard when a lot of Italian families were housed here in the fifties and sixties. They came to Alderney to help with a lot of construction work that was happening on the island".

"Oh I see" Luis replied.

"I know just the spot" Ben said. "Follow me" and off he strode. The group followed Ben across the courtyard and through a gap in the stonework to the left.

"Up here" Ben said as they all clambered up the grass back. The ground then levelled out to reveal a vast grassed area, sloping upwards to the left following the gradient of the hill and completely flat straight ahead.

"This grass looks as if it's been mowed recently" Chloe said.

"Yeah, the local Wildlife Trust try to keep places like this looking reasonably tidy for the visitors" Lilly replied.

"Look at these" Alex shouted, who by now had walked further on ahead.

The group caught up with Alex who was studying two semi circular areas marked by stone set in the ground. Running parallel with the stone were, what looked like, railway lines.

"Arh" Lilly said. "These were batteries built in the second world war by the Germans. They had two big guns situated up here which were rail mounted so that they could point them in different directions across Platte Saline beach and beyond".

The group stood there momentarily in their own thoughts as they gazed out over to Platte Saline and beyond to the horizon, an occasional gust of wind from the North disturbing their hair.

"This is perfect" Luis said. "Let's get these tents put up", and with that, they set about their task.

The two tents were up and they were quite big, easily able to accommodate the groups' bags leaving enough space to sleep three in each tent comfortably.

"So us girls will have this tent then" Chloe said, pointing to the one on the left, "And you boys can have the other".

"Fine" Alex answered. "Are we going to do a bit of exploring now?" he asked. "We need to keep an eye out for any wood so we can have a bit of a fire later on. It'll help keep us warm tonight".

"That's a great idea" Ben answered. "But we must be extra careful in there" pointing over to the main building. "Some of the flooring is really dodgy".

"We'll split up shall we" Lilly asked, "Luis, do you want to come with me?"

"Too right I do Lilly" Luis answered, his face not able to conceal his delight at the thought of being with Lilly by himself.

"Course he does" Chloe grumbled. She was totally peeved off as she'd fancied her chances with Luis. *Damn it,* she thought.

"Come on Ben" Usha called, "Lets go down here" as she pointed to the flight of stone steps that led down to the basement. It was like an external corridor that ran from one end of the building to the other, about one hundred metres in length.

Alex and Chloe had found another gap in the low wall in which another flight of stone steps took them down to the basement. "Be careful Chloe" Alex said, "There's a loose stone in this step".

"So what" Chloe snapped, "Don't care".

"Don't be like that" Alex said with a reassuring tone in his voice.

"It's always the same Alex" Chloe grumbled, "Lilly somehow always manages to attract all the good looking guys".

"Well thanks for that" Alex grunted, "I'm obviously not good enough for you then?".

Chloe could see that she'd upset Alex. "Sorry Alex, I didn't mean it like that. I like you a lot, I really do. It's just that …."

Alex put his arm around Chloe "I know, but don't let it get to you"

Chloe kissed him on the cheek "You're the best Alex, thanks".

"Let's go across here" Luis said as he stepped out onto a stone bridge that crossed over to the main building. He half turned and held out his hand towards Lilly who instinctively grabbed hold with her right hand. *He had a gentle but strong grip* thought Lilly. They slowly sidestepped across the bridge.

"That's gotta be a ten metre drop to the basement so don't let go of my hand Lilly" Luis said. Lilly shook her head in agreement.

Luis stopped on reaching the other side. He pulled Lilly towards him. They stood there close together, first looking down at the drop below and then, for a few moments they were lost in each others eyes.

God, she smells so good, Luis thought.

Lilly's blonde hair danced in the breeze as they stood there. The sun seemed to make Lilly's steely blue eyes sparkle out of control.

This is just heaven, Lilly thought, *what a guy, those muscles, his …*

"Lilly"

Luis interrupted her thoughts. "We need to move from this spot, it's quite dangerous standing here".

You got that right, Lilly thought. "Err, oh, yes we should" she stuttered.

They both stepped into what was the stone framework of a doorway long gone. Lilly pulled her hand away from Luis' realising that her amulet was in full view.

"That looks expensive?" Luis asked, who had spotted it glistening in the sunlight.

"It probably was" Lilly replied. "My Grandad gave it to me when I was born".

"Nice" Luis answered. *That is REALLY valuable*, he thought.

"You two alright up there?" Usha called out from down below.

"We're fine Usha" Luis answered, as he spotted Ben and Usha down below in the basement. He could see them through the broken floor boards that was once a floor. "You found anything down there?"

"We've managed to collect a few bits of wood" Usha shouted.

"That's good" Luis answered, "We'll see you in a bit".

Luis turned his head to see that Lilly was stood over the other side of this huge room. She was peering out of one of the many widows that were set at regular intervals along the exterior stone wall that overlooked the road below and Platte Saline Bay in the distance. *Doesn't she look just gorgeous and what a figure,* Luis thought to himself.

"Lilly" Luis called. "How did you get over there?"

"Very carefully" Lilly joked. "You need to keep to the sides. It's the strongest part of what's left of the floor".

"Okay, I'm coming round to you. Give me a couple of minutes. Stay put Lilly".

Luis slowly and carefully side stepped around the edge of the room keeping his back to the stone walls. He was within a metre of Lilly when she offered him her right hand.

"Take my hand Luis" Lilly said reassuringly. "That last floorboard is loose".

As Luis took her hand, the floorboard underneath his feet broke away and fell into the basement below. Luis instantly felt himself falling.

"I've got you" Lilly shouted. She was holding onto the window frame with her left hand. The amulet on her right wrist began to emit a blinding green pulse and the power of the light was growing stronger. Lilly held onto Luis who was dangling below her with her right hand.

"Luis" Lilly screamed "Use both hands".

Luis swung his other arm round to grab Lillys' hand. He could feel the extraordinary strength that Lilly was exerting. Her grip was almost crushing his hands. He looked up to see Lillys' eyes were now glowing dark green, nearly black.

Lilly pulled Luis up in a micro second to stand next to her. She loosened her grip from Luis and collapsed in his arms.

"Lilly, Lilly" Luis screamed, "Oh jeez, what's going on? Lilly… Lilly, please be okay".

He knelt down and placed Lilly on the only remaining safe bit of flooring, cradling her head in his hands.

"Help" Luis shouted. "Help, anyone!" Lilly wasn't moving and Luis was beginning to panic.

A voice from below bellowed out "What's going on?" It was Alex.

"It's Lilly, something's wrong with her" Luis shouted out.

"Hang on, we'll be there in a mo" Alex shouted.

"Come on Chloe, they need help" Alex said. "We'll get the others on the way. Okay?"

"Coming Alex" Chloe replied, and they both clambered up the stone steps and immediately bumped into Usha and Ben.

"What's going on?" Ben asked.

"I think Lilly might have had an accident or something. We're not sure yet" Chloe said. She turned to Usha, "Don't worry girl, I'm sure your sis will be fine". The four of them ran to the stone bridge.

"What's happened Luis?" Ben shouted.

"I … I'm not sure" Luis stammered, clearly in shock. "Lilly's out cold and we're now stuck over here with no way out".

Ben turned to the other three. "I'm not sure what's going on but we need to get them back to this side and onto this bridge". They nodded in agreement.

"I saw four strong looking planks back down there" Alex said.

"And I've got some rope in my bag" added Ben. "Will the planks be long enough Alex?"

"I reckon" Alex replied.

"Right, you stay here Usha to keep an eye, whilst we all get the stuff" Ben stated in quite an assertive voice, and the three ran off.

Usha sat down. "You alright Luis?" she asked.

"Yeah, but Lilly" he shouted back, "I'm really worried".

"Don't be" Usha called, "She'll be fine. I've seen this happen before so try not to worry". She hadn't, but it was a case of reassuring herself as well as Luis.

The others were back. Alex took charge and they carefully slid the four planks in place over the precipice below. Luckily, the planks were long enough. Alex tied one length of rope around the planks to form a more stable platform.

"Right guys" Alex said, "You just need to try and keep these steady whilst I crawl across with this rope to secure the other end. Luis, I'm coming over".

"Be careful" Chloe said with a concerned voice.

A bit of a wobble and Alex reached the other side and tied the rope to secure the planks.

"Jeez, am I glad you're here" Luis sighed.

Lilly was still out cold which made it easier for the two lads to gently carry her to safety and they placed her on the grass. The friends sat around her pondering what to do next with worried frowns on their faces when Usha pulled a small teddy bear out of her pocket and poured water onto it. She always had it with her. Usha leant over Lilly, one hand with the teddy over Lillys' mouth and a few drops of water trickled from the teddy into Lillys' mouth. She whispered in Lillys' ear "Teddy's here". A gasp of air erupted from Lillys' mouth and she sat up. "Oh sis, you had us all worried" and she threw her arms around Lilly.

"Why are we all sat here?" Lilly asked.

The others looked at one another in bewilderment.

"Don't you remember anything Lilly?" Ben asked, "Anything at all?"

"Just standing next to Luis…and ... that's it, sorry. Why?" Lilly asked.

"Hmm, sounds about right" Chloe mumbled.

"Stop it Chloe" Ben snapped at her. "Can't you see she's confused".

"Makes two of us then" Luis said.

"Whoa, come on guys. Just be thankful we're all okay" Usha said, trying to calm the situation. She hugged Lilly again.

"You was so brave Alex". Chloe embraced him. "My hero" and she kissed him.

Alex could sense his face blushing up and he could feel his heart pounding. *Wow* he thought, *this is sort of cool.*

The group cheered and clapped.

CHAPTER 5

It was early evening and the sun was low in the clear blue sky to the west. The group had spent the afternoon exploring around the grounds of Fort Tourgis. They'd found the little sentry outposts that were dotted around connected by trenches that had obviously been dug out during the second world war. It was fascinating to see and feel history around them. They'd also been busy with their phones taking photos and making little videos.

The occasional visitor had passed through. Dressed in their all weather gear, hiking boots, binoculars and backpacks. Interesting conversations had been struck up.

The sound of the wildlife and the noise of the sea had occasionally been broken by the unmistakable drone of Dornier aircraft landing and taking off at the airport in the south of the island about half a mile away.

The teenagers were now back where they'd erected their tents earlier and the boys were busy building a small fire. Luckily Luis had some matches with him.

As the girls were putting together something to eat for everyone, Usha noticed the key that Ben had used that morning to open his Dads' store. It had fallen out of his jacket pocket.

Usha picked the key up. She took Lilly to one side. "Look what I've found" Usha whispered, carefully showing her sister the key.

"The key" Lilly replied. "It's important sis. We need to take another look in Bens store when we're by ourselves".

The girls bent down.

"Pick up that piece of granite Usha" Lilly said, pointing to a small black stone in the grass. Lilly held the key in her right hand. "Hold my hand with yours, your hand with the stone".

Lilly closed her eyes. They held hands and in an instant, Lillys' amulet emitted an orange glow to their hands and as fast as it appeared, it was gone.

Lilly opened her eyes and the girls hands parted revealing an exact duplicate of Bens key.

"Hide the new key Usha and make sure you give this one to Ben". Usha nodded and they both continued to help Chloe with the food.

It was fairly dark by the time they all gathered round the fire to eat and chat about the day.

"Who fancies a toasted marshmallow?" Luis asked.

"Oh yes!" they all shouted.

"Hey" a shout from about five metres away behind the group interrupted their jovial high spirits. "What's going on here?". the voice was closer and a beam of light from a torch scanned across their faces.

"Oh hi sergeant" Alex said, standing up. It was Peter, one of the three local policemen stationed on the island.

"Oh it's you lot" Peter replied. "Should have known" and he laughed. "No worries. Just doing my rounds in the police van and I knew you were all up here somewhere 'cos I bumped into Lillys' Grandad earlier. He said you were up here overnight".

"Right sergeant" Luis said. "Fancy a toasted marshmallow?" he asked, and they all laughed.

"Okay, I'm off then, behave yourselves and keep the noise down" Peter said and turned to go ......" Oh by the way, there's been reports of flashes of bright lights up here. Anyone seen anything?"

"No, we've not seen anything eh guys" Luis replied, and they all agreed.

"Right then, enjoy yourselves" Peter said. "I'll see you around". He strode off into the darkness.

Peter was no sooner out of earshot and Ben interrupted his friends. "Anyone fancy a can?".

"Too right" Chloe called out and they all grabbed one.

An hour later and Chloe was out for the count. She'd downed a couple of beers and had dragged herself into the tent and managed somehow to get inside her sleeping bag.

Alex, Ben and Usha were in the other tent telling jokes and generally messing about whilst looking at each others phones admiring the pictures and videos they had taken earlier that day.

"Hey you two" Alex muttered, "Take a look at this vid I recorded today".

The three of them huddled round Alexs' phone. The video played. Usha gulped in disbelief. Alex had obviously recorded Lilly and Luis earlier that day. As the events played out in front of them, seeing Lilly catch Luis and pull him to safety and the dark green pulsing lights, Ushas' mind filled with dread. Lillys' secret was out and there for all to see. Ushas' thoughts were racing with wild trepidation as she tried to keep herself together.

"That's way cool don't you think guys?" Alex said.

There was no reply from Ben, he'd fallen asleep. The after effects of the beer had taken its toll. *That's lucky* thought Usha.

"What do you reckon Usha?" Alex asked. "Be cool to upload it to the internet on YouTube or Facebook" he continued with a drunken slur to his voice.

"Err … yeah … good idea Alex" Usha stuttered. "I'd leave it though until tomorrow when you're a bit more sober. Don't want to make any mistakes with it eh?"

"Hic … good thinking Usha, I'll do that" Alex replied, and with that he turned the video off and pressed lock on his phone. "I'm gonna hit the sack anyway, my head's spinning".

"Okay Alex, I'll see you in the morning. Night Ben", *he's sound asleep* she thought and Usha dropped the store key in his jacket pocket as she stepped out of the tent. *Jeez, what are we going to do* thought Usha. Where's Lilly?

Usha spotted Lilly sat down by the fire with Luis. "Sorry to interrupt you two" Usha said in a low tone. "Can I just have a quick word Lilly before I turn in?"

"Yes, sure" Lilly replied, as the two girls took four or five steps away from Luis.

Usha whispered "We're in trouble sis, Alex took a video of you saving Luis and he's going to upload it onto the internet".

Lilly gasped, raising her hands to her mouth. "Grandad's going to have to sort this out. Send a text to him on your phone. He'll know what to do. Okay?"

Usha nodded. "I'll do this text and then go to bed, night Lilly".

"Night Usha, try not to worry. Fingers crossed and all that".

TEXT …..
Hi Grandad. There's a
Video of Lilly on
Alex's phone. Needs
deleting. Love Usha x

The last embers of the fire danced and crackled in the darkness. The air was still, the sound of gently lapping waves could be heard in the stillness of the night.

"Isn't the night sky just beautiful" Lilly whispered. "You can see every star in the sky. Look, there's the constellation of Orion and over here is the north star. You can see Ursa Major, there's loads …"

"Lilly" Luis interrupted "What happened earlier today? You saved me from falling to my death. What's going on?"

"That's very melodramatic Luis."

"But …." Luis tried to continue.

"Must have been adrenaline that kicked in" Lilly said as she rolled over to place herself on top of Luis. "Forget about it Luis" as she placed her index finger onto Luis' lips.

Luis held Lilly as she kissed him full on the lips. *This is getting out of hand* Luis thought. Here he was lying on the grass kissing and caressing a girl he barely knew.

Luis gave Lilly a gentle push to stop her advances. "Sorry Lilly, it's been a long day and I think maybe you've had a bit too much to drink".

"You could be right" Lilly giggled "Good init?" and Lilly continued to kiss Luis.

"Okay, enough Lilly. Sorry. We need our beds".

"Spoilsport" Lilly replied, "But I suppose you're right".

CHAPTER 6

"Buzz buzz, buzz buzz", Richard picked up his phone to take a look who'd text him this late at night. *Hmm* he thought to himself, *it's Usha, what does she want?*

He read the text. "Christ" he muttered. "Another mess to sort out".

Richard made his way upstairs to his computer room. He'd been a computer buff ever since the early eight bit days and knew his stuff. Through the eighties he'd been a member of a computer game hacking group that involved people from all over the world.

The hackers would have their suppliers and swappers that got hold of original copies of new releases. Richard would hack into the code to include trainers into the games. Then it was a case of distributing copies freely into the public domain. The practice ruined a lot of the software houses but in those days it was classed as harmless fun.

Over the years as technology improved and progressed, Richard threw himself into keeping up with all the techniques to enable him pretty much free access into any security system in the world. Phone technology in particular was simple fare for Richard. He viewed it as cyber hacking for the good of all.

Richard sat down and fired up the systems. Twelve screens in total connected to seven or eight computers and consoles.

Right, he thought, *concentrate.* He hadn't hacked into the phone networks for a considerable period of time, so this was going to be far from easy.

Fifteen minutes later and he was in. *Just got to figure out Alexs' password now.* He turned to another keyboard to bring up an automated program. *This should do the trick* thought Richard. "I'll just port this program over into this other computer and it should give me what I want" he mumbled.

"Gotcha" Richard whispered. "Now then, let's see what you've got Alex".

Richard scrolled through the files and …. "There it is". He ran the video.

"What the …." Richard watched what had happened earlier that day. *Lillys' powers are increasing* he thought. *We need to talk before it all gets out of hand.*

Richard downloaded the video onto a spare usb memory stick he had kicking around and then deleted the video on Alexs' phone. *Just need to check his trash can and history files*, he thought. Richard deleted all the connected files and then ran a scanning program through Alexs' phone to delete any other possible connections to the video.

Richard locked Alexs' phone and then powered down his computers. *I'll text Usha to let her know it's sorted,* he thought, *then off to bed.*

"Buzz buzz, buzz buzz, b…" Ushas' hand grabbed her phone to see that her Grandad had sent her a text…

TEXT ….
Hi Usha. Video
sorted. Need to
talk later. Love
Grandad xx

The three girls pulled themselves out of their sleeping bags. It was just coming up to seven o'clock in the morning and the sun was already midway up in the sky, its' rays heating up the tent.

"Ohhhh my head hurts" Lilly groaned.

"Mine's a bit like that this morning" Chloe replied.

"Serves you both right" Usha growled. "You shouldn't have drunk so much" and she continued to comb her hair.

Usha gave Lilly a thumbs up and Lilly nodded approvingly with a smile.

"You three getting up?". A shout from outside. It was Ben.

The three girls stepped out of their tent into the blinding rays from the sun to see the three lads were already up, and by the looks of things, they'd been up for some time as their tent had already been taken down..

"Morning sleepy heads" Luis jokingly called out. "Come and look at this. Alex wants to show all of us something on his phone before he uploads it onto the internet".

They all grouped around Alex.

"This will blow your mind" Alex said excitedly as he scrolled through his files on the phone. He began to get more frantic. "Where is it?" he yelled. "It's gone. I don't believe this" his voice increasing in volume.

"What's up Alex?" Usha said with a very calm and controlled voice.

"I had a vid …." Alex stuttered "But …. You saw it Usha last night".

"Don't know what you're on about" Usha replied. "Does anyone here know what he's on about?"

The group were shaking their heads.

"I think we all had a bit too much to drink last night Alex, including you" Luis said. "Don't you think Lilly?" he continued as he turned to look at Lilly who had a sheepish look on her face.

"You're probably right Luis" Lilly sighed. But her heart was pounding. She'd never felt like this before.

Alex put his phone in his pocket. "You maybe right, I dunno, it's just that …. Oh, forget it".

Chloe grabbed hold of Alexs' hand. "I don't care what the others think, you're still my hero" and she gave him a gentle peck on his cheek.

"Come on guys, we need to go. I've got to go to work today" Ben ordered. "Grab your things, get the scooters and we'll catch up later".

CHAPTER 7

Lilly and Usha pulled up on the drive outside their house and jumped off the scooter. Usha pulled her crash helmet off, "We had a good time eh Lilly?"

"Um, yeah" Lilly stuttered. "I'm a bit worried what Grandad's going to say and concerned about Alex. What if he blabs his mouth off what he saw?"

"And what's he going to say Lilly? Usha replied, "Nothing. And if he does, who's gonna believe him? Don't worry about him. To be honest I think you're going to have more problems with Luis. Don't you think?"

Lilly sighed …. "He's a dreamboat". Her face had lit up at the mention of his name. The sparkle was back in her eyes. "I've never felt like this before Usha. There's a connection".

"Okay, okay, I get it thanks" Usha snapped. "Stop all the drooling will you. Oh jeez, what are we going to do with you?"

"Oy! You two. Are you coming inside or what?" The girls Mum, Susan, was standing in the open doorway, hands firmly on her hips. "Well?" she shouted again.

"Sorry Mum, we're coming" Usha replied. "Come on sis".

The girls dumped the backpacks in their bedrooms and were busy getting themselves ready to go to work. Like most teenagers on Alderney, they had part time jobs when the school was closed and it was a good way of topping up their pocket money. Lilly and Usha were waitresses at one of the local cafes in town. They also helped out in the kitchen preparing food and washing the assorted pots. It was good experience, good fun and a great way of catching up with all the local gossip.

Today they had a split shift. A couple of hours in the morning and then another two in the afternoon.

"Come on you two otherwise you'll be late" Susan shouted from downstairs.

"Okay, we're coming" Lilly yelled as the two girls skipped and jumped down the stairs. They headed for the front door.

"Oh girls" Susan said, "Your Grandad phoned earlier and would like to see you, so I told him you'd both give him a visit for lunch. Alright?"

"Yeah that's great Mum, we'll do that" Usha replied. "It'll be nice to see Grandad. See you later".

The girls waved to their Mum and closed the door behind them.

"We'd better go on the scooter" Lilly said. "Especially as we're visiting Grandad later".

"That's alright with me" Usha replied. "Saves all that walking".

The girls sat astride the scooter and sped away.

The café was quiet this morning, thought Usha. Just a couple of visitors sat at the table over in the corner. *Just as well it's quiet,* Usha pondered, *'cos my sis is not on the same planet this morning.* She gave Lilly a scowled look of disdain.

Lilly was leaning on the counter and appeared to be lost in her own thoughts.

A group of twelve visitors entered the café and scattered themselves around the empty tables and chairs.

There was no reaction from Lilly as her thoughts overcame every other instinct. *I know nothing about him,* Lilly thought, *and that's the thing. It's exciting, it's thrilling. If this is love, wow! All the other girls fancy him, so why me? Why the attraction? Is it just luck? Or could it possibly be my destiny?* Her mind was racing ....

"Excuse me!" Usha growled at Lilly. "Helloooo" she yelled directly into Lillys' face. Any chance of some help here?" Usha demanded.

"Dur … oh … what's that you said sis?" Lilly muttered.

"I seriously need some help Lilly, look" snapped Usha, pointing to the crowd of visitors staring at the girls with demanding looks.

"Yeah, sorry sis. My fault. I'll crack on" Lilly replied.

Usha huffed and puffed. She started to take the orders.

Lilly and Usha were still arguing about events at the café earlier, when they arrived at their Grandads' house on the scooter.

"Okay Usha, I get it" Lilly snapped. "Let's forget it for now. We'll see what Grandad has to say".

"We certainly will" Usha muttered. "He must be in the back garden 'cos this front door is locked" continued Usha, giving up on the door handle.

The two girls wandered round to the back of the house.

"Hi Grandad" Lilly said.

"Oh hello girls. Didn't realise it was lunchtime. I've been so busy trying to build this greenhouse I lost track of time".

"You seem to be winning the battle" Usha said.

Richard put his screwdriver down and got up off his knees. "Right girls, let's get off inside up to my computer room and we'll have a chat. We don't want to be too long as your Grandma will be back from the shops later and you'll both be wanting lunch. No rest for the wicked" he joked.

The three of them entered the computer room and Richard powered up one of the consoles.

"Lilly, could you pass me that vase from there" Richard asked, pointing to the window sill on the far side of the room. Lilly gave him the vase and Richard tipped it up on end. The usb memory stick dropped into Richards' hand. "Can't be too careful eh?"

The girls nodded in agreement.

Richard inserted the usb memory stick into the console and found the file he'd downloaded from Alexs' phone the night before.

"Sit down girls and watch this". The video played and there was a stunned silence as the events with Luis and Lilly played out. "I've not seen that happen before," Richard said, "Not even using my amulet, so we've a few issues to deal with".

"Just recently, I've been feeling more 'connected' with the amulet" Lilly mused. "I can't explain it. Every time I use it I feel more powerful. The thing is, is it dangerous?"

"I don't know the answer to that Lilly but there has to be an explanation. We need to find out what's going on before you lose control" Richard replied.

"So, what DO we know?" Usha asked.

"Well I've never told either of you the story that goes with the amulets or your little teddy Usha so I think now would be a good time" Richard explained. "Just remember, a lot of this is based on legends and myths. Some of this story was related to me some years ago by my friend Dave who's no longer with us sadly".

"That's who used to have that store down at Fort Tourgis" Lilly interrupted.

"Yeah that's right". Richard nodded and smiled.

The girls were transfixed as their Grandad continued to explain how two or three hundred years ago, privateers plundered and shipwrecked many ships around the Channel Islands, including Alderney. They were, in essence, pirates that had permission from various governments to raid ships of their valuable cargoes.

Many of the ships used by the privateers were financed by local island families such as Le Mesurier and Carteret. That is why many consider the Channel Islands to be wealthy countries.

In 1820 the Treasure of Lima which they think could now be worth about £200 million was taken from Lima in Peru to Cocos Island just off Costa Rica to be buried for safe keeping.

In 1832, the ship Jupiter sailed from Peru to Hamburg in Germany and on its return trip to Lima the following year it was shipwrecked on the rocks north west of Alderney. Apparently the soldiers aboard were thrown into jail and the Jupiter was looted by local privateers. Many believe that the Treasure of Lima which included gold statues and jewelled stones went down with the ship whilst some locals in Alderney think that some of it, if not all of it, was brought to shore and hidden.

The jewelled stones of the Treasure of Lima were reputed to possess mystical powers especially when strung together with gold braid to form amulets and were part of the Incas' treasure that were stolen by Spanish soldiers during the wars in South America in the early nineteenth century.

Richard went on to explain.

"Dave had some good contacts in the antique trade in the islands and he gave me these two amulets that he'd been given a good thirty or so years ago. He reckoned there had to be more but he never said where".

"I've worked out that the different colours of the jewelled stones or crystals obviously have different powers". He continued.

"The white crystals gives off a white halo and possess' some sort of healing powers".

"Yeah, but I've found out" Lilly interrupted, "That it must give off some sort of electrical current 'cos I got a dead light bulb to power up".

"Interesting" Richard said. "The red crystal, as we know, gives off a red halo and seems to make things disappear. And now we know the green crystal emits a dark green halo and seemingly super human strength. Mind you, the dark green eyes are not a good look Lilly" he joked.

"The one thing I do know about the crystals is they are precious stones" Richard explained. "I'll have to do some research online and get back to you. In the meantime, you need to be careful, especially when you're with your friends". He gave the girls a knowing look.

"Your teddy is an interesting story Usha" Richard said. "I've just got time to explain before we have lunch".

The girls listened intently as their Grandad told them the story.

"As you know, I was born in Wales. In 1977 there was an exhibition that included the wooden Nanteos Cup which was rumoured to have been made out of the cross that Jesus was crucified on.

Anyway, it went missing for a while and when it was returned it was slightly damaged. They didn't make too much fuss at the time as they were so relieved to get it back.

The teddy was given to me by my Great Grand Father with the strict instructions to never get it wet because it was stuffed with wooden shavings. Years later, my mother told me that apparently the riddle of the missing bits of wood from the Nanteos Cup was explained by the fact my Great Grand Father repaired the cup and used the shavings to stuff the teddy.

The legend goes that the Nanteos Cup had supernatural healing powers when drunk from it".

"That's what happened with Lilly" Usha interrupted.

"What?"

Usha continued "Up at the Fort. Lilly was out for the count. She was barely breathing after she collapsed. I soaked teddy with some water and wet her lips with it. Lilly immediately recovered".

"Amazing" Richard said. "The legend is true then. You need to take great care of that teddy Usha".

Usha nodded in agreement.

"So the cup behaves a little bit like the fabled Holy Grail?" Usha asked.

"I suppose it does" Richard replied. "Don't go thinking that makes you both invincible, in fact, you need to be more careful than ever until we can figure out what we're really dealing with. I'll get online as soon as I can to see if I can find any more information.

"Hello …. Hello up there" a shout echoed through the house.

"That sounds like your Grandma girls. Time for lunch eh?" Richard said. "Better look sharp or you'll be late back to work".

CHAPTER 9

Annie Dodds was busy sorting out the returned library books which had built up over recent days when she caught sight of Chloe sat down on the floor in front of one of the sets of book shelves in the corner of the library.

Anne summoned Chloe over with a wave. "Miss Chloe Mollins" she growled "I know you only work here on a part time basis but a little more effort would be appreciated".

"Sorry Mrs Dodds".

"Well quite" Annie grumbled. "Here, I've sorted these returned books out alphabetically, so if you wouldn't mind putting them back on their correct shelves, it would help. Okay?"

"I'll get on with it now" Chloe replied, picking up a stack of the books and she turned to go with a soulful look on her face. Her heart wasn't really in it. She hated the job and only did it to help her Mum out financially. Her Dad had died a couple of years ago in a car accident and she missed him dreadfully. Chloes' heart was broken but she'd stayed tough not only because of stuff that had been said to her at school, but for her Mum as well.

Annie beckoned Chloe back and put her arm round her. "Chloe, I'm sorry, I didn't mean to upset you. I know what you've been through and you know that you only have to ask if you need any help or advice" Annie reassured her.

"Thanks Mrs Dodds, that means a lot" Chloe replied and smiled briefly as she carried the books over to the shelving.

"Hi Annie. How are you?"

Annie turned to see Richard standing at her counter. "Oh hello Richard. Haven't seen you in here for some time" Annie said with a slight tremble. She'd always had a bit of a thing for him even though he was married.

"Well, you know how it is" Richard replied. "Busy, busy, busy".

Annie nodded in agreement.

"You still giving Chloe a hard time then?" Richard joked as he winked at Annie.

"No ... no, not at all" she whispered. "It's just, you know how these youngsters are, but Chloe's a good girl who just needs a bit more support than some of the others, you know".

Richard smiled and nodded reassuringly. "You're right of course" Richard added. "Anyway, I'm here 'cos I'm after some sort of reference book. Anything to do with shipwrecks and that sort of thing around the seas of the Channel Islands, in particular Alderney. Lilly's doing a project for school and I said I'd help her out. Do you think you might have something?" *Another white lie* he thought.

"I'm sure we will" Annie replied, "In fact, Chloe's tidying that section right now.

"Thanks Annie, I'm sure Chloe will be a big help" and Richard sauntered off towards the girl.

"Hi Chloe, how are you doing?" Richard asked. "Did you enjoy yourself with Lilly and her friends yesterday?"

"Oh hello Mr Morgan. Yeah it was good thanks" Chloe replied "And I think your Lilly has found herself a new admirer". There was a glint of mischief in Chloes' eyes.

"Who's that then?"

"His name's Luis Garcia" Chloe said, "He's fairly new to the island. His dad's a plumber you know and Luis works full time with him".

"Does he now" Richard muttered. "So I guess he's older than Lilly then?"

"I think he's seventeen" Chloe sighed.

Richard paused for a moment .... "Hmm ... right then. Err, I'm looking for some sort of reference book about shipwrecks. Perhaps you know where to look?"

"You need to be looking over there in the corner Mr Morgan". Chloe pointed to the top shelf of the shelving unit.

"Thanks Chloe, I'll take a look .... Oh, and say hi to your Mum for me will you".

Chloe smiled and nodded to Richard. She picked up the books and carried on organising the shelves in front of her.

This row of reference books are covered in dust, Richard thought. He spotted what looked like the very one he needed ... Shipwrecks in the Channel Islands 12th-19th Century. *Perfect*, he thought.

Richard sat down at one of the five available tables. The book was quite old with some water damaged pages but all the text and maps were still legible. *Strange as well,* he thought, *this book isn't dusty unlike the others on the same shelf.*

Inside the front cover there was only one date stamp. *This book has only ever been taken out of the library once and that was over twenty years ago,* Richard thought, *this is weird.*

Richard quickly flicked through the pages from back to front stopping at one in which the corner had been creased over as a marker.

"That's interesting" Richard whispered to himself. The page was information about the ship Jupiter which had sunk near Alderney in 1833. It also went on to list what cargo it was shipping and there it was .... Lima Gold. *Bingo,* Richard thought, feeling pleased with himself.

Richard ran his fingers across the page and he caught the corner marker, turning it to it's normal position revealing a hand written number. "Number 77" Richard whispered to himself. *It has to be a page number* he thought. He quickly turned to the page to reveal what looked like an extract of the ships log. It listed names of sailors that were on board that fateful day in 1833 and one name and his nationality was circled in pen.

"Garcia …. Peruvian" Richard gasped. "It surely can't be" he whispered and slammed the book shut.

"Everything alright Mr Morgan?" Chloe enquired. She was stood immediately behind Richard.

"Oh, yes thanks" Richard replied, thinking to himself, *how long has Chloe been stood there? Did she see what I was looking at?* "Could you put this book back for me Chloe? And could you do me a favour?" he continued. "Would it be possible for you to find out who took this book out previously for me please? It's about twenty years ago, a bit before your time I know, but there should be some sort of record. Thanks".

"Yeah sure Mr Morgan"

"Great. There's no rush. If you don't see me around just send me a text. Alright young lady?"

Chloe nodded and smiled as Richard left the library saying goodbye to Annie as he did so.

CHAPTER 10

The two girls were coming to the end of their afternoon shift at the café and were busy cleaning out the fridges and washing pots. It had been very quiet and they'd only served a handful of customers, so they had taken the opportunity to discuss the implications of the amulets and Ushas' teddy. They were both excited and fearful at the same time, wondering where the situation would lead them.

Usha continued wiping down the tables and clearing away the few remaining pots and cutlery whist keeping an eye out for potential customers.

Lilly was in the back kitchen preparing vegetables and the like, to put in the fridges ready for the following days menu and was in a world of her own. She was listening to music on her iphone using her headphones and as she worked, Lilly was moving and singing along to the music.

Ushas' concentration was interrupted by the sight of two scooters pulling up outside the café. It was the three boys. Alex hopped off his scooter and was first to enter quickly followed by Luis and Ben who looked decidedly bedraggled.

"Hope you lot have got clean boots" Usha growled. "I've not long mopped the floor".

"And hello to you too" Alex snapped.

"Sorry Usha" Luis and Ben said in unison. "We've both been working at the same house" explained Ben "And we've just finished. Thought we'd drop in and grab ourselves some pasties and a bottle of coke".

Luis nodded in agreement scanning the café for any sight of Lilly.

"You looking for Lilly?" Usha enquired.

"Err ... yeah" Luis stuttered with an embarrassed voice.

"She's through the back in the kitchen" Usha sighed.

Luis leapt over the counter and entered the kitchen. *What the ...* he thought, here was the girl he thought he knew, singing and dancing with all her heart oblivious to his presence.

He recognised the song. It was Eternal Flame by The Bangles. *Lillys' voice was great,* he thought, as she continued to sing ….

"Close your eyes, give me your hand, Do you feel my heart beating, Do you understand, Do you feel the same, Am I only dreaming, Or is this burning an eternal flame".

Luis put his hands on Lillys' hips and she spun round to face Luis with a startled look which quickly changed into a huge smile. She pulled the headphones from her ears as Luis held her closer and they melted together.

Lilly started to sing again with Luis joining in as they danced together. *This is just heaven,* Lilly thought.

As the song finished, the two of them held each other tighter and kissed each other passionately.

Ben, Usha and Alex stood in the doorway clapping, whistling and shouting encouragement, when a voice from the front of the café boomed "Hey! You lot, what's going on?". It was Richard.

The three teenagers stood aside with sheepish looks as Richard strode over to the entrance of the kitchen.

Lilly and Luis were still kissing. "What do the two of you think you're doing?" Richard yelled.

They separated and turned towards Richard. "Grandad" stuttered Lilly "we …."

"We what?" Richard asked.

"Nothing" Lilly said. She felt embarrassed.

"Sorry Mr Morgan" Luis mumbled, "It was just a bit of fun. You know." He turned to Lilly "Sorry Lilly, I'd better go". Luis squeezed Lillys' hand and marched out of the kitchen turning to Ben as he did "You coming Ben?" The two lads left the café.

"I'd better get going as well" Alex said, "I promised Chloe I'd pick her up from the library".

He clambered onto his scooter and he was gone.

Usha placed her arm around Lilly. "Come on, we need to finish up and get off home" Usha whispered.

Richard had left the kitchen. "Okay" Lilly replied, "But I know a quicker way. Stand back". Lilly touched the orange crystal on her amulet. She closed her eyes and in an instant an orange halo materialised and disappeared. The kitchen was spotless.

"That's a bonus" Usha joked. They both grinned.

Meanwhile, Chloe was just leaving the library after her shift had finished when Alex pulled up on his scooter.

She ran over to him and threw her arms around him. "Oh Alex" she sighed "I'm so pleased to see you" and she kissed him on the cheek.

Alex could see that her eyes were teary. *She's having one of her bad days,* he thought. "Come on girl, hop on behind me. You can have tea at my place if you like. My Mum's got the day off from the hospital so she won't mind cooking for an extra mouth".

Chloe nodded and smiled. She'd always been fairly close with Alex and since her father had died, he'd been a great shoulder to cry on with all her problems. She jumped on the scooter and put her arms around Alexs' waist as he pulled away.

Alex and Chloe arrived at his house. It was an imposing building. His Dad had built it a few years earlier and it was in a prime situation at the top of the road that cut straight through the middle of the local golf course.

Alex parked the scooter on the drive and immediately went over to his For Sale box to see how many golf balls he'd sold that day. The box was empty and his money box was full with money. *Cool,* he thought, *the money will come in handy.* "Fancy helping me look for some more golf balls Chloe?"

Chloe replied "Yeah, why not".

"Okay, give us a minute" Alex said, "I'll just let Mum know what we're doing and I'll grab the dog. We can give him a walk at the same time". Alex was in and out of the house in a flash, the dog bounding along behind him.

"Right, come on" Alex said, "Let's get going 'cos it'll take a couple of hours to look round the golf course. Oh, and my Mum says you can stop the night if you want. She's already phoned your Mum to let her know.

Chloe gazed and smiled at Alex. "You're the best" she said, and kissed him on the cheek.

It was a long walk, but the teenagers didn't care as they chatted about life and general stuff. Chloe felt more at ease in those moments than she had done for a few weeks. They stopped for a rest and sat down on one of the benches that were dotted around the golf course.

"Do you think there's something weird going on with Luis?" Chloe asked.

"Not sure I know what you mean girl" Alex replied. "I reckon something is going on, but I can't put my finger on it. It's like this afternoon, Lillys' Grandad came in the café and sort of lost his cool with Lilly and Luis. Not really what you expect from Mr Morgan 'cos he's always been pretty cool with all the kids."

"That's strange" Chloe replied. "Mr Morgan was at the library earlier today. He was nice, as he always is, but he was acting rather strangely. He was studying a reference book about shipwrecks. It just seemed odd because he very rarely comes in and when he does it's usually just for a chat with me or Mrs Dodds".

Chloe continued "And the really weird thing about it was that he asked me to find out who had taken that book out 'cos it's only got one date stamp on it. Something's going on".

"Did you find out?" Alex asked.

"I didn't have time today" Chloe sighed, "But I need to look in the records when Mrs Dodds isn't there".

"Well if you need me to help just ask" Alex said. "We need to get to the bottom of this I reckon. It could be important .... I do think Lilly is involved with all this. Why else would her Grandad lose his temper this afternoon? And I still remember filming Lilly and Luis up at Fort Tourgis"

"You still going on about your lost video?" Chloe interrupted. "Come on Alex, you was drunk".

"Yeah but …"

"You was drunk Alex. Forget it" Chloe snapped. "Sorry mate, I didn't mean to shout at you" and she kissed him on the lips.

Alex wrapped his arms around her as they caressed and kissed before rising from the bench.

"Come on, let's go and see what my Mum's cooked for tea" Alex said. They called out for the dog and strolled home hand in hand.

CHAPTER 11

Lilly rolled over in her bed and through half closed bleary eyes she caught sight of her clock. Nine in the morning …. *Jeez,* she thought, *need to get up.* Luckily she didn't have to go to work that day. She quickly got dressed. She brushed her hair as she made her way down stairs and into the kitchen.

"Oh hi sis" Usha said, who was in the process of finishing her bowl of cereals. "Mum and Dad have gone to work. Mum said they'd be out all day so we'd have to sort ourselves out for lunch".

"Right" Lilly said, "I'll get something to eat then. What are we doing today?"

"Well I know that Ben's working with his Dad over on the other side of the island" Usha answered, "So how about we go and take a look around his Dads' workshop. We've got the key." Usha held the copy of the key up.

"Good idea gal" Lilly replied. "I'll get myself sorted and you pack some stuff together. Don't forget a torch, just in case, and we'll get going."

The girls straddled themselves over onto the scooter. Just then, their Grandads' van pulled up.

"Here we go" Lilly muttered, "More trouble and strife." Usha sighed.

"Here's my two princesses" Richard called as he made his way over to them and pecked them both on their cheeks.

In unison, the two girls replied "Hi Grandad."

"I'm glad I've seen you both this morning. I've got something to say. I just wanted to say sorry to the pair of you about having a go at you yesterday at the café. I was bang out of order. I don't want to spoil your fun and you're both old enough to be responsible for yourselves, if you know what I mean."

The girls nodded.

"The one thing I would say Lilly is just to be careful when you're with Luis. Okay?"

Lilly smiled.

"Right, on that note, I'm going. Love you both" and Richard gave them a hug.

"Catch up with you later" and Richard waved to the two girls as he drove off in the van.

"Right sis let's get going" Usha muttered in Lillys' ear and the scooter sped off spluttering as it disappeared down the road.

Five minutes later and the girls arrived at the parking area at Platte Saline.

"We'll leave the scooter here" Lilly said "And we'll walk round the corner of Fort Tourgis to Bens' workshop."

Usha nodded in agreement and continued "Probably for the best, then we won't draw attention to ourselves".

The sisters picked up their bags and headed off down the lane. Their hair danced from side to side as the wind hit them in their faces as they turned the corner before reaching the wooden door of the workshop.

The girls glanced around to make sure no one was looking and Usha put the duplicate key in the door and turned it. Clunk, it worked and the door creaked, as if it was relieved to be released from its' bonds.

Lilly pushed the door open and the girls stepped inside.

"Close the door Usha" Lilly whispered "And I'll sort the light out." Lilly closed her eyes and concentrated momentarily, visualising the light bulb. This was the first time she'd tried using her powers without touching her amulet.

Usha interrupted Lillys' thoughts "That's enough Lilly, the light's dazzling me. Turn it down before it explodes" she shrieked.

Lillys' eyes opened to see the room bathed in white light. Usha was knelt down with her hands shading her eyes.

"Ha, that's pretty good" Lilly laughed.

"I'm impressed Lilly, but next time, try it with your eyes open so you've got more control" Usha growled. "But at least now, you seem to be getting more of a handle of what you're capable of."

"Yeah, it's going to take practice I suppose" Lilly replied.

"Lock the door Usha, just in case."

The greater distribution of light than their previous visit revealed a much larger area in the workshop than before. The floor was thick with countless years of dust and the girls could tell it was a combination of gravel, concrete and floorboards depending on the sound beneath their feet.

The surrounding walls and roof were solid granite rock slowly narrowing further back in the workshop. The various shapes of the rock indicated that this place had been tunnelled out by hand probably by a few poor souls in the second world war.

Rubbish and antique style tools and machinery were scattered around the workshop, some barely distinguishable as the cobwebs had virtually hidden them.

"What exactly are we looking for Lilly?" Usha asked with a discernable disinterested tone of voice.

"I don't know" Lilly replied, "It's just that I felt some sort of connection with this place when we were here the other day with the guys." Lilly continued "And then when Grandad mentioned about his friend who'd died and the fact that he'd given him the amulets, plus Ben had said his Dad had been given this place by Grandads' friend."

"So there must be something here sis" Usha said, "But what?" Usha shrugged her shoulders.

"Just keep looking Usha" Lilly answered as both girls moved slowly towards the far end.

"How about you try 'connecting' with your mind and the amulet?" Usha asked. "I know you've never done anything like this but surely it's worth a try?"

Lilly sighed … "Okay, I'll give it a go. Stand back just in case something goes wrong."

Lilly stood in the middle of the floor and raised both hands to waist height, her palms away from her. She closed her eyes and cleared her thoughts. Lilly concentrated on an image of her amulet in her head and suddenly she was no longer in control of her thoughts.

Usha watched intently as the amulet on Lillys' wrist started to glow all the colours of the rainbow and then vibrate. *Had Lilly lost control*, she thought.

Lilly opened her eyes which were now glowing jet black in a scarily sort of way and she slightly turned to face Usha.

Usha suddenly lost all control of her movements and watched helplessly as Lillys' amulet glowed with increasing intensity.

Usha started to walk in a zombie type of way. She had no control of her own movements and could do nothing as Lilly seemingly was controlling her.

In front of her, Usha could see something glowing rhythmically in time with Lillys' amulet. Ushas' arm rose up, still under Lillys' control, and her hand grabbed the object in the wall. She pulled it towards her and in that moment the two girls were released from whatever force they had both experienced.

"Lilly" Usha shouted, "You okay?"

"Yeah, I think so. Are you?" Lilly asked.

"Pretty much" Usha replied, "Come and take a look at this". She pointed to the object in the stone wall. "It looks like some sort of statue that's been made into a lever. Awesome".

"Wow, it looks like an Inca figure" Lilly exclaimed, "And look what's happened over there in the floorboards. It's a trapdoor. The lever must have opened it.

The two girls studied their discovery and lifted the trapdoor to reveal a rope attached to the underside and hand hewn steps leading down to …

There was a noise at the wooden door.

"Usha, grab the bags and the torch and get down there" Lilly whispered, pointing to the trapdoor. "I'll get the light" and instinctively Lilly powered the light off. *Getting good at this,* she thought.

The girls clambered down the steps below the floorboards and pulled the rope to close the trapdoor behind them.

"Stay perfectly still Usha. Don't say a word and keep the torch switched off" Lilly whispered.

The wooden door to the workshop swung open, creaking and grinding as it did. The space was engulfed in sunlight.

"Right Ben, don't hang about." a voice shouted.

The girls squirmed and cringed as they hid below. It was Ben and his Dad, Mr Allens.

"Okay Dad, but where are they?"

"There should be a couple of toolboxes near the back wall. Here, I'll help you".

The two of them walked across the floorboards, sending dust through the holes and cracks onto the girls below. It seemed like forever as the girls looked at each other trying to stay calm.

"Got them" Ben called.

"Good lad. Let's get going then 'cos we don't want to be wasting any more time on that job".

As the big wooden door closed, the sisters breathed a sigh of relief.

"Phew, that was close" Usha whispered. She switched her torch on.

"Wow, look around Usha" Lilly muttered.

Usha waved the torch around to reveal a small room with a low tunnel running off in the direction of Fort Tourgis.

"We need the proper gear on Usha to go any further" Lilly said, "Look, there's water further down the tunnel".

"You're right" Usha replied, "Another day then". She turned to head back up the steps to the trapdoor when the light from her torch caught a glimmer of something below the steps. "What's that?" as she held the beam of light still, to let Lilly see the object.

Lilly bent down and moved her hand across the floor. "Got it". She dusted the object off. "It's a pendant on a chain Usha. I wonder". and she passed it to Usha.

"Let's get out of here" Usha said and the girls pushed on the trapdoor and clambered out.

Lilly quickly powered the light back on. "That was so close" she said. "I thought they were supposed to be working at the other end of the island today".

"So did I" Usha replied. She took another look at the pendant they'd found. "This crystal looks the same type as those on your amulet. It's a dark reddish colour. I wonder if the chain is gold?" Usha hung it round her neck. "Should look nice when it's been cleaned up".

Lilly nodded in agreement. "So what exactly happened to me sis?"

The girls sat there for a few minutes describing to each other what they saw and felt.

"It's amazing Usha" Lilly said. "I seem to be getting more powers and gradually achieving some sort of control over them just by using my mind, or sub conscious, or something like that".

They both laughed.

"You don't really know do you?" Usha joked.

"Come on, let's go. I'm hungry" Lilly beckoned to her sister. "We've got everything? Lilly asked. "I'll sort the light, you get the door".

The two girls stepped out into the daylight and locked the wooden door behind them.

They slowly walked hand in hand back down the lane towards Platte Saline. The sun was at its' hottest time of the day, high in the sky and looking to their left the girls could see two fishing boats bobbing up and down out in the bay. The colour of the sea was a mix of blue, indigo and almost black as they turned the last corner into the parking area where they'd left the scooter.

"Is that Grandad sat there?" Usha asked, pointing over to the small grassy bank which formed the boundary between the parking area and the beach in Platte Saline Bay.

"It sure is" Lilly answered, having already spotted Richards' van parked further away.

As the sisters drew closer they could detect the smell of fish and chips. "Gawd, I feel hungry sis" Usha muttered. Lilly nodded in agreement.

Richards' head turned as he heard the girls footsteps and he smiled. "Good to see you both" and he gave them a bag of fish and chips. "Thought you'd be hungry. Your Mum told me you were looking after yourselves today and I spotted the scooter. So I called in at the chippy at the harbour. I took a chance that you wouldn't be too long before you appeared. So tuck in girls".

Lilly and Usha sat down either side of Richard to devour their lunch. They were so hungry and it was rather nice to be sat there eating with the lapping of the sea and the expanse of sand in front of them.

"So where have you two been this morning?" Richard asked, "Because I've tried phoning you a couple of times and getting no answer".

The sisters jumped at the opportunity to tell their Grandad of the mornings' adventure.

"An exiting development then" Richard exclaimed. "Tell you what, come up to my place this afternoon and I'll show you what I've found out. We'll take a look at the pendant as well eh, Usha. Your Grandma will be out so we'll be okay".

CHAPTER 12

It was early afternoon when Lilly and Usha arrived at their Grandads' house. Richard was busy in the back garden topping up the bird feeders. He'd normally do it first thing every morning but he had immersed himself on the internet trying to find any other information that tied in with the Lima Treasure and any possible connections with local families. As always, Richard had lost track of time when he was on his computers and what with meeting up with the girls earlier, his time had flown by.

"Hi Grandad" The two girls called as they walked into view.

"Hi girls, what's new?" he replied.

The girls shrugged their shoulders.

"Help yourselves to a drink out of the fridge, I'll be with you in a mo" Richard said, "Just got to finish dealing with these bird feeders".

The sisters disappeared into the kitchen to grab the cold drinks.

"Here you are Grandad" Lilly said, as they stepped back into the garden. "We've got you a drink as well".

"Oh thanks girls, let's sit down on the bench shall we? And I'll tell you what I found out at the library".

The three of them sat on the bench under the weeping willow tree. The tree gave a welcome dappled shade in the hot afternoon sun. It was a favourite place for Richard. He would often sit and watch the variety of birds as they helped themselves to the bird food he'd provided.

Richard explained to the girls how he'd found a book in the library which gave details of the shipwreck in the early 1800's and that it had as part of its' cargo the Treasure of Lima. It was listed in the Captains' Log as Lima Gold. Richard then continued to tell the girls how one of the sailors involved in the shipwreck was Peruvian. His surname being Garcia.

"That's Luis' surname" Lilly interrupted.

"Yeah I know" Richard replied. "It could be just coincidence, but…." and he paused "To be honest girls, I just don't know. We might have a bit more of a clue if young Chloe can find out who took that book out of the library twenty years ago".

"Hang on! What? How come Chloe's involved?" Usha snapped. "She's a bit of a loose cannon".

"Hold it right there young lady" Richard replied. "Yes, she's had her problems over the last couple of years or so, but she's a good girl at heart. I'm disappointed in you Usha, you should be trying to help her instead of throwing accusations around".

Richard continued "Anyway Lilly, this is why I told you to be careful when you're with Luis. It could be nothing".

"I do believe there's some connection" Lilly said. "I can really feel something when I'm with him".

Usha raised her eyebrows and gave Lilly a stare.

"What's that look for?" Lilly asked.

Usha sat there giggling.

"Right" Richard said, "Let's take a look at this pendant you found.

Usha handed the pendant to her Grandad. "It's a bit grubby" she said.

"Don't worry, we'll soon have it sparkling like new. Let's go in the old shop store and I'll sort it out" and Richard beckoned the two girls to follow him into the store.

Richard had built the store years ago, across the length of the back garden to enable him to store goods for the convenience shop he used to run before he retired. These days it was full of tools and machinery which he used when he repaired other peoples lawn mowers and pretty much anything that was motorized.

"Get the lights please Lilly" Richard asked.

Without thinking, Lilly obliged in an instant as the store lit up.

"I'm impressed. You're going to have to show me how to do that 'cos my amulet is identical to yours Lilly" Richard said as he walked over to one of the benches and switched on a buffing machine. It was actually a grinding wheel that he'd changed to use as a polishing wheel.

Richard carefully handled the pendant and chain as it was buffeted by the wheel, stopping occasionally to judge which part to polish next. It didn't take long and he switched the machine off.

"There you go Usha" Richard said as he handed her the pendant "As good as new I reckon. The chain is definitely gold, the same as the amulets, and the crystal … what a beauty. What do you think Usha?"

"Wow Grandad, that's excellent" Usha replied, "And the colour is stunning. Such a deep red. That's brill, thanks". Ushas' face lit up and she was smiling from ear to ear.

"I take it you're happy then?" Lilly asked.

"It's really cool eh" Usha answered. "The thing is, what does it do?"

The three of them laughed.

"I'm sure you'll find out at some point gal" Richard said, "And that's the point, none of us really know what each crystal does".

"Well, that's not strictly true Grandad" Lilly said, "I mean, they obviously work together like when I was able to control Ushas' movements in Mr Allens' store".

"Yeah, I get what you're saying Lilly" Richard said, "But each crystal must have, or transmits, different powers and it's going to take time to find out as and when you use these powers".

The girls nodded in agreement.

"One thing I do know for sure is that each time I use my amulet, the strength and power exerted appears to feel stronger. It's going to take practice to be able to control these powers so I don't hurt anyone" Lilly said.

"Exactly" Richard added.

"So, let's see what you can do Lilly" Richard said, "But just be careful".

"Okay" Lilly replied and she took two or three steps back from Richard and Usha. She closed her eyes and cleared her head of any thoughts. Lilly visualised the amulet and immediately sensed she was in control. She opened her eyes that were now glowing white. Lilly turned slowly and as she felt the surges of energy flowing through her body, she lifted her hands, pointing them at the various electrical tools on Richards' work bench. The tools burst into life creating a cacophony of noise and the lights in the store were flashing on and off.

Richard stood open mouthed and in awe at what he was witnessing whilst Usha jumped up and down clapping and laughing.

The noise subsided as Lilly lowered her hands and the machinery spluttered to a halt.

"Awesome" Usha shouted.

Lilly's eyes returned to normal. "How was that?" she asked.

"Yeah … err … well, what can I say" Richard stuttered. "So is that what you intended to do Lilly?"

"Pretty much" Lilly replied "Each time, I seem to get better control".

"How about trying something else" Richard suggested. "Let's go back into the garden".

"This is going to sound a bit naff" Richard said. "Usha, get some empty tin cans out of the recycling bin and line them up on that table in front of the wall".

"You've been watching too many cowboy films" Usha joked as she placed the cans on the table.

"You're kidding me, right?" Lilly asked.

"No" Richard replied. "Just stand about five metres away and see what you can do to each can".

Lilly shrugged her shoulders and faced the cans. "Ready?" she shouted.

"In your own time" Richard shouted.

Lilly closed her eyes and concentrated on her image of the amulet in her mind and as she felt the energy building up, she raised her hands and opened her eyes to reveal the usual glowing and..... Nothing.

What the? She thought.

Richard and Usha watched with interest.

I'll try something slightly different, Lilly thought. She repeated her usual technique, but this time she raised just one hand and as the energy built she threw her arm forward in a thrusting motion.... Clang! The first can went flying. With another thrust the second can flew away.

Usha by now couldn't control herself as she laughed, shouted and jumped up and down. "Yeah, go Lilly". Usha lost control of her next jump and she faltered towards and in front of the tin cans and at that moment, Lilly sent a power pulse hitting Usha, sending her flying across the lawn three metres away.

"Lilly stop" Richard yelled as he ran to Usha. "You alright gal?"

Usha rolled over, giggling with a big grin. "Awesome" Usha said.

They all started laughing.

"Are you sure you're alright sis?" Lilly asked.

"Yeah, course I am" Usha replied, "why?"

"'Cos the pendant you're wearing is pulsing" replied Lilly with a concerned look on her face. "Can't you feel it?"

Usha glanced down at the pendant around her neck to see it throbbing red pulses of light.

Richard and Lilly looked at each other and then glanced at Usha who was about to touch the pendant. "Don't!" they both instinctively shouted ....

In that moment, Usha had grabbed the pendant. She stood there fully surrounded by, what looked like, some sort of energy field. It was the height of Usha and glowed red.

"Awesome" Usha shouted with a huge grin on her face.

Richard picked up one of the empty tin cans and threw it directly towards Usha. The can hit the energy field and flew off over the wall into the neighbours' garden. *Wow*, Richard thought.

"Try moving an arm Usha" Lilly shouted.

Usha stretched one arm out and turned around on the spot. The energy field immediately covered a larger area surrounding Usha.

That's incredible, Richard thought. "You'd better let go of the pendant now Usha" Richard shouted.

Usha loosened her grip on the pendant and it stopped pulsing, dispersing the energy field at the same time.

The three of them stood there momentarily stunned and then burst into cheers and laughter.

"Hmm, right" Richard said. "It looks like the power pulse from Lilly must have hit your pendant Usha, bringing it back to life so to speak".

Usha nodded in agreement.

"Could you see both of us through the shield sis?" Lilly asked inquisitively.

"Yeah, sure, why?" Usha replied.

"Well, I don't know about you Grandad, but all I could see was the shield" Lilly said.

"You're right Lilly" Richard replied, nodding in agreement. "It was as if you wasn't there Usha".

"Awesome" Usha shrieked. "Like being invisible".

"I wish" Richard joked. "Right then, you two need to go 'cos it's school tomorrow and your Grandma is due home about now. Just remember what I said, be careful, at least until we know more".

The two girls nodded and waved their goodbyes as they left their Grandads' house in an excited mood.

CHAPTER 13

Alex and Chloe had been having a fairly lazy morning watching a couple of videos and listening to their favourite music from a huge collection of CD's that Alex had accumulated over the years. It had been great for Chloe, after staying the night, not to have to deal with her family issues. She hadn't felt this much at ease since before her father died a couple of years ago and life certainly had picked up over the last two days as she and Alex had become closer.

"I really ought to be going Alex" Chloe whispered in his ear as she snuggled up a bit closer on the sofa they were sharing. She kissed him on the cheek. My Mum probably needs a hand with some of the chores before she goes to work. She's on the afternoon shifts this week 'cos the hospital are short of staff.

"Sorry Alex" Chloe said as she lifted herself up from the sofa, "I really must go".

"Yeah I know" Alex replied. "Give me a couple of minutes to sort out and I'll give you a lift home". Alex left the room.

"Mum" Alex shouted, "I'm going out for a while. I'm going to give Chloe a lift home".

Alex popped his head round the door "You ready gal?"

Chloe nodded and followed him out of the house waving to Alexs' Mum with a smile.

As they clambered onto the scooter, Chloe said "Can you thank your Mum for me when you get back Alex?".

"Yeah of course" Alex replied, "She likes having you here anyway. Girly talk and all that" he joked.

A few minutes later and the scooter pulled up outside Chloes' house. Most people knew where she lived because the garden had been left to do its' own thing since her father died. It was very overgrown and definitely needed a bit of muscle.

Alex and Chloe approached the front door which was slightly open.

This looks a bit odd, Alex thought. "Let me get the door Chloe" Alex said. He grabbed the door and pushed. The door stuck halfway. Alex peered around the door and to his horror saw Chloes' Mum sprawled out on the floor.

Alex glanced back at Chloe "It's your Mum Chloe …. she's out for the count".

Alex and Chloe squeezed though the gap of the partly open doorway. Alex closed the door behind them to give the pair of them more room to move.

"Oh Mum, what have you done?" Chloe sobbed as she knelt down by Carol, her Mum.

"Chloe … Chloe" Alex said with an assured look on his face, "I think she's just passed out 'cos she's drunk. Can't you smell the drink on her?"

Chloe nodded and continued to sob uncontrollably.

"We need to move her" Alex said, "So we can try and help her. Chloe … are you listening?"

Chloe stood up wiping away the tears from her face. "Nearest room is the lounge" Chloe sighed. "We'll have to see if we can move Mum onto the sofa".

"Okay" Alex said "I'll get hold of your Mum under her arms and you get her legs. Just take it nice and easy".

Luckily, Carol was quite slim and not too tall and the two teenagers eventually managed to manoeuvre her onto the sofa, propping her up slightly between the armrest and the back.

"I'll get some black coffee on the go" Chloe said as she disappeared into the kitchen.

Alex knelt down and started to gently tap the cheeks of Carol. "Mrs Mollins ... Mrs Mollins ... Hello. Come on" Alex muttered quietly. He didn't want to scare her. *She's obviously been drinking in this room,* thought Alex. There was empty bottles strewn about the floor. Partially filled glasses and broken glass were randomly dotted around the room. *Some serious drinking,* Alex thought.

Chloe stepped into the room and placed a cup of coffee on the small side table next to the sofa. She had a blanket under her arm. "How's Mum doing?" Chloe asked as she tenderly placed the blanket over Carol.

"Mum. Mum" Chloe said as she stroked Carols' hand.

Carol stirred and slowly opened her eyes.

Chloe threw her arms around her Mum and kissed her on the cheek. "Oh Mum" Chloe whispered "You're gonna be alright. Don't worry".

"I ought to go" Alex said. "I think your Mum will be alright once she's sobered up".

Chloe stood up and hugged Alex. "Thanks Alex. I don't know how I would have managed without you" and she kissed him gently on the cheek.

"No worries" Alex said. "I tell you what, I promised Ben that I'd pick him up from work, so I'll call back round later to see if everything's okay".

"That'd be nice" Chloe replied and kissed him again.

Alex disappeared from view out of the front door.

Chloe glanced at her watch. *Jeez,* she thought, *Mum was due at work half an hour ago. I'd better phone them to let 'em know she won't be in,* Chloe thought.

Chloe found the hospital number on her phone and dialled it. After a couple of rings someone answered at the other end. "Alderney Mignot Hospital. How can I help?"

"Oh hello" Chloe said "My name's Chloe Mollins and I'm ringing on behalf of my Mum, Carol. She isn't very well and she won't be able to come in to work today, sorry".

"Right, thanks for letting us know Chloe. Hope you're Mum's better soon" replied the voice on the other end of the phone.

Chloe hung up.

"What the hell do you think you're doing?" Carol shouted in a drunken slur. She'd been stood behind Chloe for the duration of the phone call.

Chloe turned to face her Mum, whose eyes were full of hatred.

"How dare you tell them I'm not going to work" Carol shrieked with venom.

"But Mum ..."

Carol staggered, managing to stay upright with the aid of the wall. "And who was that with you?"

"Mum, you know who ..." Chloe said.

"Don't you give me any lies" Carol interrupted with a menacing voice. "It was some boy wasn't it? You little tramp!" Carols' voice was raging. "I bet he's only after one thing".

Chloe tried to say something. Anything. But her Mum was out of control. The alcohol was in control.

"You're a tramp" Carol raged. "A tart" Carol shouted and as she ranted out of control, Carols' arms and hands were swinging at Chloe.

"Mum. Don't. You're hurting me" Chloe cried out, but still the blows kept landing. Chloe finally lashed out to defend herself and Carol slumped to the floor.

Chloe turned and fled out of the front door in floods of tears.

Alex pulled his scooter on to the gravel parking space by the side of the lighthouse. He'd drove round to the north eastern side of the island to pick up Ben who'd been helping his Dad on a carpentry job, fitting a new kitchen.

Alex sat there admiring the lighthouse. He'd never really studied it before. The lighthouse is also known as the Mannez Lighthouse and was constructed in 1912 using local granite stone. It has a height of 37 metres. *Impressive,* Alex thought.

"Hi Alex" a voice interrupted his thoughts.

"Oh, hi Ben" Alex replied. "You been busy?"

"Just completed the job, it looks good" Ben said. "Do you know, we had to go to my Dads' store today for a couple of toolboxes. Haven't been there in months and now twice in two days ... ha! It was strange though. I could have sworn that someone else was there. Obviously not, but it just seemed weird at the time".

"Right" Alex said "Hop on. I've just got to call in on Chloe on the way 'cos I promised"

"That's fine" Ben replied.

By the time the two lads reached Chloes' house, Alex had told Ben about how he'd found Chloes' Mum. They screeched to a halt on the driveway.

Chloe was lying on the driveway face down and motionless.

"Chloe" Alex shouted, as he jumped off the scooter and ran to her. "Ben, check in the house for Mrs Mollins".

Ben dashed past Alex and Chloe into the house, his heart thumping heavily in his chest. He reappeared almost instantly "We need an ambulance Alex. I'll phone now".

Alex gently turned Chloe over cradling her head in his hands. There was so much blood. *How long had she been lying here? Why did I leave her?* Thoughts were racing through his mind.

Ben knelt down besides Alex and put his arm around his shoulders. "Keep thinking positive thoughts mate" Ben whispered. "She'll be alright. She's a survivor".

Alex nodded to his friend as tears rolled down his face. "If anything happens to Chloe ..." Alex sobbed.

Ben interrupted "It won't mate. The ambulance is on its' way. I can hear it".

Alex tenderly kissed Chloe on the cheek. He ran his hand across her forehead to try and move some of the blood matted hair that was stuck to her face. "Oh Chloe" he sobbed as he rocked her back and forth like a baby.

"Excuse me, we need to get through" a voice from behind interrupted Alexs' crying. Ben pulled his friend away from Chloe to let the paramedics work on the girl.

"Mrs Mollins is in the house" Ben shouted. "She needs help as well"

By now, two or three people had assembled on the driveway to see what all the commotion was all about.

"Come on now, give these people some room to work in" a voice boomed through the crowd. It was the local sergeant,

Peter Cordy. He approached the two lads. "Come with me boys, there's nothing more you can do here".

"But sergeant".

"No buts. I'll take you up to the hospital for a quick check up and then we'll see how Chloe and her Mum are when the ambulance gets' them up there, okay?"

The boys nodded and followed Peter.

An hour had passed. The boys had been checked over and had given statements to the sergeant with Alex also giving details of the events at Chloes' house earlier that day.

Ben was pacing back and forth across the waiting area in the hospital whilst Alex was sat silently in his own thoughts.

They'd been told that Mrs Mollins was sobering up in a private room. She had no injuries but had been sectioned, which meant that they would be flying her out to the larger island of Guernsey to receive treatment and counselling at the major hospital.

Alderney is one of a group of islands that fall under the legal jurisdiction of Guernsey.

Chloe was in the intensive care unit and was being monitored constantly.

The main entrance doors opened. Luis, Lilly and Usha walked in accompanied by Richard. The three teenagers gathered round Ben and Alex whilst Richard went off to find someone to see how Chloe was.

Richard eventually found a nurse. It was Alexs' Mum, Mrs Bean. Coincidentally she was covering the shift that Chloes' Mum should have been working.

"Hi Beth" Richard said, "How's young Chloe doing?" he asked.

"Not too good I'm afraid" Beth replied. "Such a shame 'cos she's a really nice girl when you get to know her. She was at my place this morning you know, 'cos she's taken a shine to my Alex. It's hit him hard I think".

"I'm sure it has" Richard replied.

Beth continued, "Lots of scratches and bruises, but".

"But what?" Richard asked.

"She must have received a blow to the head" Beth said. "There's been internal bleeding and a blood clot has formed in her brain".

"Meaning what?" Richard asked with a concerned look on his face.

"It means" Beth replied, "If the clot doesn't disperse in the next couple of hours, it could leave her paralysed".

Richard gasped. He thanked Beth and returned to join the teenagers who were trying to cheer Alex up. Richard whispered in Lillys' ear "I'm going outside, follow me in a couple of minutes". Lilly smiled in acknowledgement.

Richard walked out of the main doors.

"I'm just going outside to see where Grandad is" Lilly said as she walked out through the doors.

"What's this all about Grandad?" Lilly asked.

Richard told Lilly exactly what Beth had told him a few minutes earlier. "We have to try and help" he added.

"But how?" Lilly asked. "Neither of us know if I'm able to do that sort of thing".

"I know Lilly" Richard replied. "If it is possible, it means that you've literally got to get inside her head. It's dangerous but I feel that we have to try".

"You do know Grandad, that if it works, Chloe might remember something" Lilly said, as she held her Grandads' hand for reassurance.

"It's a risk we're going to have to take Lilly" Richard said. "Do it. I'll go and find Nurse Bean to see if she'll let a couple of you sit in with Chloe".

Lilly and Richard walked back inside the hospital. Lilly went back to her friends in the waiting area whilst Richard disappeared down one of the corridors to look for the Nurse. Five minutes later he returned with Beth.

"Alex. Lilly. Come with me please" Beth said in a softly spoken voice and she led them down the corridor to the intensive care unit. "Right then you two, don't worry about all the equipment attached to Chloe." Beth spoke softly as she continued, "Just sit either side of her. You can talk to her but she won't respond physically because she's heavily sedated. The experts always say that the patient can hear you, so it does give them some comfort and assurance that a friend is there with them".

Beth pushed the door open. "There you go guys. I'll be back in a little while" Beth said.

"Thank you Mum" Alex said and the teenagers walked to Chloes' bed.

Lilly gasped and put her hand to her mouth as the enormity of the situation dawned on her. Chloe lay there motionless with various different tubes and sensors attached to her. She was covered in bruises notably around her eyes and her head was bandaged where she had obviously suffered a bad head wound.

Alex sat down to the left of the bed and tenderly held Chloes' hand and started whispering to his girlfriend. Tears were rolling down his face.

Lilly handed Alex a tissue. "Here Alex, take this" in a very quiet voice. She sat down close to Chloe to the right of the bed and held Chloes' other hand gently.

Lilly reached out and tenderly placed her right hand on Chloes' right cheek. She breathed deeply and cleared her mind of any thoughts. Again, she took a deep breath as she lowered her head to hide her eyes from Alex. She concentrated on the image of her amulet in her mind and then instantly she could see what Chloe was thinking. For a moment, Lilly thought she was imagining the images and thoughts, but no, what she was seeing was events that had happened between Chloe and her Mum earlier that day. *This feels like I'm in Chloes' dreams,* Lilly thought.

Lilly could feel her eyes pulsing and her power was increasing. She delved deeper into Chloes' brain and suddenly she 'felt' the arteries and veins flowing around Chloes' brain. *There it was, the blood clot.* Lillys' thoughts were massaging the arteries around the blood clot …. and then it released itself as the blood flowed through into the blood starved brain. Lilly could see the nerves healing and the electrical impulses kick starting the brain into life.

Lilly moved her hand away from Chloes' face and she gasped as the amulet relinquished its' power.

"You alright Lilly?" Alex asked.

"Err … yeah I'm fine" Lilly replied as she lifted her head. "Must be tired, I keep nodding off. I tell you what, I'll leave you two alone for a while" and Lilly stood up to leave.

"Alex. Lilly". Chloe murmured.

"Oh Chloe" Alex whispered "I thought I'd lost you".

Lilly smiled, "I'll see you guys later" and she left the room feeling euphoric.

Lilly entered the waiting area and beamed a big smile towards her Grandad. He nodded approvingly.

"Chloes' going to be alright" Lilly exclaimed, unable to control her voice.

The four friends couldn't conceal their delight as Luis wrapped his arms round Lilly and kissed her passionately. Ushas' smile on her face couldn't hide her delight that Ben had put his arm around her shoulders.

Richard stood there silently. *My Granddaughters are growing up,* he thought.

"Come on guys" Richard said. "Fish and chips are on me. Let's go down to Braye Chippy".

"What about Alex" Ben asked.

"His Mum is going to take him home when she's finished her shift here at the hospital" Richard replied. "Besides, he wants to stay with Chloe".

"Here you go guys" Richard said as he passed the portions of fish and chips round.

It was a glorious evening, sat at the diners tables outside the chippy. Richard sat there quietly thinking about the days' events, whilst the four youngsters were discussing Chloe and her predicament.

"I'm off then" Richard announced. "Who wants a lift home?"

Ben and Usha shouted "Yes please".

"Is it alright if Luis gives me a lift Grandad?" Lilly asked.

"I'll make sure she's not late" Luis added.

"That's fine" Richard replied. "Just remember it's school tomorrow".

Richard clambered into his van and beckoned Usha and Ben. The three waved as the van pulled away.

"Your Grandad's alright you know" Luis said. He put his arm round Lilly.

"Yeah, he's the best" Lilly replied. She kissed Luis full on the lips and they were both lost in the moment.

"Come on gal" Luis whispered in Lillys' ear. "I'll take you home. It's been a long eventful day".

CHAPTER 14

"Time for school girls" Susan shouted upstairs.

"We're coming Mum" Usha replied. She picked up her school bag and peeked round Lillys' bedroom door. "You ready sis'?

"Yeah, sure" Lilly replied. *Have I got everything I need for the exam?* she thought. Lilly was in her final year at school and today was her last day and her last exam.

The two girls bounded down the stairs, jumping off the final two steps into the hallway.

"How many times do I have to tell you?" Susan shouted "Don't jump off the stairs like that, you'll hurt yourself".

The sisters looked at each other and started giggling. "Sorry Mum" Lilly said. "We'd better get going, you coming sis'?"

"Okay girls, I'll see you later. Good luck with the exam Lilly" Susan said.

"Lilly, are you working at the café after school?" Susan asked.

"Yes Mum, but I'll finish my shift in time to pick up Usha. Okay?"

Susan hugged both girls before waving to them as they left on their scooter.

It was a two minute journey down Braye Hill to St Annes School, the only school on Alderney. The girls waved to friends they passed, who were walking to school.

What a lovely morning, Lilly thought. The air was crisp and clear with blue skies all around. The sea, which was visible across Braye Bay directly in front of them glistened in the sun with three or four various shades of blue.

"It's like a mill pond out there today" Usha shouted to Lilly. "Too nice for school" she joked.

The girls parked up outside the school and made there way inside, casually chatting to friends they passed.

"Right Usha" Lilly said, "You have a good day. I'll pick you up this afternoon after school".

"You too sis' and do your best in the exam" Usha replied. The girls hugged and headed off in opposite directions to find their lockers.

Lilly had her head in her locker. *Where's that ruler?* she thought, *and I need a spare pen.* "What the…" Lilly squealed.

Two hands had gently grabbed her waist from behind. She spun round to face Luis who instantly kissed her. *Wow* thought Lilly.

Lilly eased Luis away slightly. "Luis, you shouldn't be here" she whispered. "If any of the teachers see you, they'll kick you out. You need to go now or they'll be trouble".

"Well there's gratitude for you". It was Alex who was stood slightly behind Luis. "I did tell him Lilly, but he wouldn't listen".

Lilly threw her arms around Alex and kissed him on the cheek. "Alex, I didn't think I'd see you today".

"Exam!" Alex replied. "Last one, same as you". Lilly nodded. "Luis picked me up on his scooter 'cos mine's broke down and he was passing my place on his way to work".

"How's Chloe?" Lilly asked.

Alexs' face lit up. "She's gonna be alright. Just needs rest now".

"I think we need to make a move" Luis interrupted. "We seem to have attracted a crowd".

The three friends glanced around to see that they were surrounded by at least twenty other students.

Lilly spotted two teachers approaching down the corridor. She grabbed hold of Luis and kissed him passionately on the lips. Luis could feel his face reddening up with embarrassment as the crowd cheered and clapped.

"Gotta go" Luis muttered "Good luck both of you in the exam" and he squeezed through the crowd of pupils and ran off down the corridor to the exit.

Alex and Lilly sat down. They were in the school hall with about twenty other students for their final exam of the year before leaving school for the last time.

The two friends were both sixteen and both in their final year at school. These exams would determine their future in terms of employment or further education, which a lot of the kids preferred. To carry on their education it meant studying for A level qualifications in Guernsey. This would mean leaving Alderney which Lilly was far from happy about. Alex on the other hand eventually wanted to go to university which meant he would have to achieve his A levels first.

"Right everybody" a voice from the front of the hall. "Good morning. You have two hours for this maths exam. Good luck. You may start now."

"What a relief" Alex sighed, as he sauntered out of the school hall with Lilly. "I'm glad that's over with.

"Yeah, bit on the tough side" Lilly replied.

Lilly glanced down the corridor to see it was completely blocked with students.

"What's going on down there?" Alex said. "Come on, let's take a look".

The two friends walked towards the crowd of students who by now were shouting and muttering between themselves.

"That's your Mum there Alex" Lilly shouted as she pointed towards the middle of the crowd.

"What's she doing here?" Alex asked.

Lilly shrugged her shoulders.

The other students stepped away from each other allowing Lilly and Alex to walk through to see Chloe and his mum stood in the middle of the melee looking totally perplexed.

"Mum. Chloe. What the…" Alex stuttered.

Chloe stepped forward shakily and threw her arms around Lilly.

Lilly was frozen to the spot momentarily. "Chloe" she mumbled.

"Lilly" Chloe whispered in Lillys' ear. "Lilly, you saved me…. You really did save me".

Lilly tried to compose herself. She could see tears were running down Chloes' swollen and bruised face.

"Chloe, you're confused" Lilly whispered.

"Mum, what are you doing here?" Alex asked.

"The hospital discharged Chloe this morning" Mrs Bean explained "Providing she stays with us, being as I'm a nurse. I was taking her home but she was insistent on coming here first to see Lilly. I've no idea why. Do you know why Lilly?"

"No. Sorry Mrs Bean. I really don't know" Lilly stuttered.

"Right then. Come on Chloe" Mrs Bean said. "There's been far too much excitement this morning young lady. You coming Alex? 'cos I can give you a lift seeing as your scooter has broken down".

"Yeah, okay Mum" Alex replied.

Alex turned to Lilly and kissed her on the cheek. "You at the café later?" he asked.

"I'm on my way up there now" Lilly replied. "Just got to collect all my books, get the scooter and I'm away. I'll see you later maybe".

CHAPTER 15

It was lunchtime and the café was busy with local workers and tourists. The place was heaving and Lilly had been left by herself. *Not for the first time*, Lilly thought.

"Any chance of some service over here?" boomed a voice from over in the corner.

"Yeah, I need another cuppa over here darlin'" another voice shouted.

There was muttering and moaning about the service to be heard in every direction as Lilly struggled to keep her composure. She was flustered and could feel her anger at being left in this situation building up when the door flew open.

It was Luis. He stood there and glanced around immediately realising his girlfriend was being hassled. He was only seventeen, but he was a strapping young lad with a physical presence. The murmurings subsided as he walked over to the counter and kissed Lilly on the cheek.

"You got problems gal?" Luis said loudly, making sure everyone in the café heard.

"Oh Luis. Am I glad to see you." Lilly sighed. "Any chance you can help?"

"Yeah sure. But I'm not exactly dressed for it." Luis joked as he looked himself up and down in his scruffy boiler suit.

"No probs" Lilly replied and threw him an apron. She grinned at him lovingly.

"You gotta be kidding me" Luis gasped as he tied the apron around him.

Lilly giggled and blew him a kiss.

"What do you need me to do?" Luis asked as he placed his hands on his hips in disgust.

"You clear the empties from the tables" Lilly continued "And take to the kitchen. Then take the orders whilst I serve here at the counter and prepare any food for orders".

"Is that all madam" Luis said with a huge grin.

"It won't be for long" Lilly replied. "The café will go quiet after lunch. About an hour".

"Hmmm" Luis picked up an empty tray and went over to the tables.

Lilly busied herself with the job in hand, occasionally giving Luis a big admiring smile. *He's all mine*, she thought.

Lilly sighed with relief. It had been hectic for the last couple of hours.

"My hero" Lilly purred as she threw her arms around Luis and kissed him on the lips.

The two remaining customers at the tables smiled and looked away.

The pair sat down at one of the empty tables for a well deserved drink. They had no sooner settled when Celia Perez, the reporter from the local weekly paper, entered the café accompanied by a cameraman. She walked up to their table, microphone in hand.

"It's Lilly isn't it?" Celia asked as she pushed the microphone purposely forward. "Lilly Gat. That's right isn't it?"

"Who's asking?" Luis interrupted.

"It's alright Luis" Lilly said. She held his hand to reassure him and herself.

"Yeah, that's me … and?" Lilly asked.

"Perhaps you could comment on the incident at Mrs Mollins' house yesterday involving her daughter Chloe?" Celia asked.

"Not really" Lilly replied. "I wasn't there was I ... and you know that surely from the Police report if you're doing you're job right eh?" Lilly said quite sternly as she looked Celia directly into her eyes.

"You was there at the hospital though" Celia pressed on.

"And? Chloe's my friend. I went to see her" Lilly replied. *I can see where this is going,* Lilly thought and she held Luis' hand a little tighter.

"Apparently Lilly, I have it on good authority that you was present in Chloes' room when she made a miraculous recovery" Celia asked as she pressured Lilly further.

Lilly squeezed Luis' hand a little more and she could feel her heart pounding faster in her chest.

Celia pounced on Lillys' hesitation. "This isn't the first time is it Lilly?" Celia asked.

Lillys' eyes glanced at Luis. He had the look of someone who also wanted an answer.

"I have no idea what you're talking about" Lilly said with a faltering voice. She took a deep breath. "It's just a coincidence that I was there. If you have information on so called good authority, then show me what proof you've got".

"But ..."

"Thought so" Lilly interrupted. "You're following up on an Alderney rumour. You're clutching at straws for a story that doesn't exist". Lillys' voice was getting more confident. "As for your comment of 'you have it on good authority', well I'm sorry, you haven't, 'cos everyone at the hospital has to sign a confidentiality agreement. I have nothing further to say on the subject".

"Lilly. I'm just doing my job" Celia said.

"Yeah. Not very well it seems" Luis intervened.

"You're digging for something that isn't there" Lilly added as she released Luis' hand and stood up. "I need to close now" Lilly said. "Luis, do you mind getting the door for these two?"

Celia turned to Lilly as she stepped out of the café. "I'll be keeping an eye on you".

Luis closed the door. "Do you mind telling me what that was all about" Luis said.

Lilly placed her hands on Luis' waist. "It's nothing Luis, absolutely nothing" and she kissed him on the cheek.

Lilly could see there was a look of doubt in his eyes.

"Look, if it makes you feel any better, think about it. You was at the hospital as well. I went to see Chloe and sat with Alex. He never left the room. Ask him yourself if you don't believe me. I left before Alex. End of".

"It's not that I don't believe you" Luis said "It just sounds a bit odd if you know what I mean and all of a sudden we've now got a reporter on the case".

"Luis please, I don't want us falling out over this. It's just silly nonsense" Lilly said "Come on, hold me tight and give me a kiss".

The pair stood there for a moment lost in their passionate embrace when Lilly suddenly remembered about having to pick Usha up from school. Lilly glanced at her watch over Luis' shoulder.

"Sorry Luis, I need to go right now" Lilly whispered in his ear. "Got to pick Usha up".

Lilly was sat on her scooter outside the school. She was lost in her own thoughts as she waited for Usha. She was worried about Chloe. She was worried about Luis. She was also concerned about Celia. *What if? What if? What if?* Her head was swimming with different scenarios.

"Lilly. Lilly" A shout interrupted her thoughts. It was Usha. School was out and crowds of students were heading home. Lilly spotted Usha mingling in and out of the crowds. Lilly waved to her sister.

"Over here Usha" Lilly shouted.

Usha hugged her sister.

"Had a good day sis'?" Lilly asked.

"Yeah. Sure. Can we just go?" Usha demanded.

The sisters drove off on the scooter.

As soon as the school was out of sight, Lilly felt a nudge in the back. "Pull over" Usha shouted.

The scooter slowed to a stop and Lilly turned to Usha. "Come on, what's up?" Lilly asked.

"School, that's what" muttered Usha "And so called friends" she added.

Usha continued "There's been all sorts of stuff going round the school about you Lilly. Some of my friends have even called you a witch. It's all over the local social media. What are we going to do sis'?"

Lilly placed her arm around her sisters' shoulders to reassure her "Not sure sis'. Let's go and drop off your stuff at home. Then we'll go and see Grandad to see if he can help sort this mess out" Lilly said.

The two girls arrived at Richards' home.

"I bet he's working round here" Usha said as they turned the corner of the house.

"Grandad" Lilly shouted.

"Over here" Richard replied. He was bent over in the corner pruning a few of his rose bushes. He stood up to see where the girls were stood and as he did so, he caught himself on one of the rose thorns, gouging a deep scratch in his arm. "Ouch. You bug…" he shouted in pain.

"Language Grandad" Usha shouted.

Blood was pouring down Richards' arm. "Let's take a look Grandad" Lilly said.

Richard held his arm out, and before he could do or say anything, Lilly passed her hand over his arm and it was healed.

"Hmmm, thanks Lilly" Richard muttered.

"How did you do that Lilly?" Usha asked.

"Don't know" Lilly replied. "It just seemed instinctive".

"I'm not being funny Lilly, but you've got to stop doing this sort of stuff", Richard said. You just don't know who's going to be around. You've got to be more objective as to how you use these powers. Do you understand what I'm saying?"

"You're right Grandad" Lilly replied. "But at the time, it seems the right thing to do".

Richard smiled. "I know". He continued, "Anyway, why the visit?"

Usha started to tell Richard what was going on at school.

Richard interrupted "Tell you what, let's go for a walk and you can tell me all about it".

As the three of them sauntered off down the road, Usha picked up where she left off and explained to Richard what had been happening at the school.

"Okay, as I see it, the first thing to do is sort out the social media stuff" Richard said, "It's a big ask, but I'll try and fix all that tonight when I get on my computers".

Usha smiled and put her arm around Richards' waist as they walked further down the road.

"Chloe knows I helped her" Lilly stuttered.

"What" Usha said.

"What" Richard exclaimed, "Mind you, we knew we were taking a chance".

"Well, at least, I think she knows" Lilly said. "She visited the school earlier today with Alexs' Mum and she said that I had healed her. The thing is, when I sat with Chloe at the hospital, I saw images and her thoughts of what had happened earlier that day. I couldn't help it. It just happened".

Usha looked at Lilly in a knowing sort of way.

"So I'm guessing now" Lilly continued, "But do you think it's possible that at that moment, Chloe knew it was me in her thoughts?"

"I suppose so, but we're not going to know for sure are we" Richard replied.

"There's something else as well" Lilly said, "That reporter woman, Celia Perez, was at the café this afternoon and she was digging. She reckons she's got inside information from the hospital".

Richard sighed.

"Right okay" said Richard, "Girls, for the moment you're going to have to bluff 'em out. Be careful what you say if anyone asks. In the meantime I'll try and catch up with Alexs' Mum, the Nurse, to see if I can find anything out. And just give Celia a wide berth for now 'cos believe me, she's an interfering busy body".

"Chickens!!" Usha shouted.

"What the …" exclaimed Richard.

Richard and the girls had been so preoccupied in conversation, they'd walked into the field where the chickens were kept. They all laughed as the birds surrounded them demanding food.

"Okay girls, it's time for you to go. Your Mum and Dad will be wondering where you are" Richard said, "And it looks like I've got a busy night ahead on my computers".

The two sisters gave Richard a big hug and ran off.

It was the following morning and Beth was trying to wake Alex up. "Alex. Alex" Beth shouted.

Alex stirred as he turned over on the sofa he'd slept on overnight, to see his Mum stood over him. He glanced at his watch and could just make out the time through his sleepy eyes. He stretched out his arms and yawned.

"Mum, it's half past five in the morning" Alex grumbled.

"I know what time it is my lad. You need to be up and about 'cos I'm due in work at six". Beth continued, "You've got to be up to look after Chloe. She's still in bed getting some much needed rest, but she's still very shaky on her feet".

"Okay Mum". Alex pulled himself up onto his feet. "Don't worry, you get off to work".

Beth smiled and kissed Alex on his forehead. "You're a good lad", Beth said as she stepped out of the house.

Richard was on a mission this morning. He'd been busy throughout the night on his computers, sorting out his grandchildrens' concerns on social media. It had been complicated. Now he needed to find out what problems there were at the hospital, if any. *Need to do it without drawing any suspicion,* Richard thought.

Richard pulled the van into the hospital car park. *Pretty quiet,* he thought as he climbed out and sat down on one of the garden benches that surrounded the car park. He glanced at his watch. *Nearly break time for the nurses,* Richard thought.

The main door of the hospital entrance opened and two nurses walked out, cups of tea in hand. Richard spotted Beth.

"Hi Beth" Richard shouted. "Fancy a chat?" he asked.

"Yeah, why not" Beth replied. "What brings you here?" she asked.

"Just came to ask how Chloe was doing" Richard replied.

Beth smiled. "She'll be okay. Still very shaken up though" Beth added. "Did you know that she had a severe head wound Richard?" Beth asked.

"No I didn't Beth. All I knew was what you told me the other day when I brought her friends up to the hospital" Richard replied.

"It's just that" Beth said, "I shouldn't be telling you any of this Richard".

There was an uncomfortable pause.

Richard gently held Beths' hand.

"Beth, I've known you since you was knee high to a grasshopper. I've watched as you've grown into a young mother with a family to be proud of. And you have a very important job." Richard said in a caring sort of way.

"The thing is" Beth said, "After you and Chloes' friends left, the consultant in charge that day, called in to monitor Chloes' progress. After removing her head bandage to inspect the wound, it was if nothing had been there, unbelievable. He also checked the monitoring machines that were attached to Chloe, to look at the read outs. Apparently there was some sort of an anomaly at about the time her blood clot dispersed when young Lilly was sat alongside Chloe with my Alex".

"And that proves what?" Richard asked.

"Well, nothing really" Beth replied. "It just seemed very odd at the time" she added.

"Who was the consultant?" Richard asked.

"You're really pushing your luck Richard" Beth replied. "It was Dr Perez" she stuttered.

"I had a feeling it would be him" Richard replied.

"Why?" Beth asked.

"Have you looked at social media from yesterday?" Richard asked.

Beth gave Richard a quizzical look.

"Obviously not" Richard said. "Typical Alderney scenario that takes only one comment to spark a debate off and generally coming up with the wrong answers. And you know who's stirring it up? Dr Perez' daughter, Celia".

"The reporter?" Beth asked. "The doctor should know better. He shouldn't be telling his daughter anything, especially with the job she has".

Richard nodded in agreement.

"Look, I need to go Beth" Richard said.

"Yeah, and I need to get back to work" Beth replied as she glanced at her watch.

"Beth. Thanks for the info" Richard said. He turned to go. "Hand on heart Beth, what you've told me, stays with me and if I was you I'd watch yourself with Dr Perez".

"I know" replied Beth. She walked back into the hospital.

Richard breathed a sigh of relief and he returned to his van.

Better call in at Lillys' place, Richard thought.

CHAPTER 16

Usha was at school. She'd left her sister in bed earlier that morning, zedding! It was break time and Usha had her head in her locker looking for books for her next lesson when she felt someone standing close behind her. She glanced round to see Ben who had a smile as big as the proverbial Cheshire Cat.

Ben placed his hands around her waist and kissed Usha on the cheek.

"Hi" Ben said.

"Oh hello Ben" replied Usha. *Awesome,* she thought.

Usha closed her locker and held Bens' hand. "Let's go and sit down over there for a minute" Usha said, as she pointed over towards a bench.

The two youngsters pushed themselves through the students, who were seemingly walking back and forth aimlessly.

They sat there holding hands in a slightly embarrassed way.

"What lesson have you got next?" Usha asked.

"History" Ben grunted. "I hate History. What have you got?"

"English," Usha replied. "I hate English".

And the two friends burst into laughter and together they said "I hate school".

Usha began to feel faint.

"Usha, are you alright?" Ben asked. "All of a sudden you look dreadful" he said in a concerned voice.

Usha could barely hear Bens' voice. Everything was becoming a blur. But what she could feel was her pendant pulsing underneath her school blouse. She could feel herself falling, or so she thought.

Ben could barely contain himself.

"Usha" Ben shouted, "What's happening?"

Usha was now prostrate on the corridor floor. A crowd was gathering around the two friends and she could feel herself slipping from consciousness. Then, blackness. Somehow, Usha was connecting with Lillys' thoughts. *How can this be,* she thought. *Lilly needs my help.* She knew it, she could feel it, and now …. Usha could see what Lilly was seeing.

Lilly was still in bed at home. She was in a dreamlike state. Her amulet was pulsing and taking her to an unknown place and Lilly seemed to be not in control. She was able to think, and her visions were almost in black and white, blurred around the edges. *Lilly was with Chloe*, or so she thought. And then she realised what she was seeing. Chloes' dreaming.

Lilly could see Chloe and her Mum fighting again, as she had done when Lilly had saved Chloe at the hospital. But this time she spotted something in the hand of Chloes' Mum. A bottle of pills. *So that's why Mrs Mollins had been so violent. She was high on drugs as well as being drunk.*

What happened to the pills? A thought popped in Lillys' head. It was Usha. *Find the bottle Lilly,* another thought from Usha. Lilly realised that somehow, Usha was communicating with her.

Lilly saw Chloes' struggle continue and then, there it was. As Chloe lashed out at her Mum in self defence she knocked the bottle out of her Mums' hand. She picked it up and stuffed it in her pocket before she staggered out of the front door and collapsed on the drive.

Where are the pills now? Lilly couldn't see them and Chloes' dream was becoming fainter. *What's happening to her?* Another thought from Usha.

Lilly concentrated on her power and then she saw the bottle next to Chloe. Lilly looked closer, there was a name on the bottle. P E R ... Perez, and it was empty. *Oh jeez,* she thought. *Chloes' took all the pills. She's taken an overdose and she's .... she's dying. Help her Usha.*

Lilly woke up in a cold sweat as the amulet relinquished its' control.

In the same moment, Ushas' pendant stopped pulsing and she was conscious. She sat up surrounded by a crowd of students and Ben was knelt beside her holding her hand.

"Jeez gal, what was all that about?" Ben asked in a concerned tone of voice.

"How long have I been out Ben?" Usha asked.

"A few seconds, you must have fainted" Ben replied.

He helped Usha to her feet as the crowd dispersed. *Awesome,* she thought.

"Ben, phone Alex and get him to check on Chloe", ordered Usha.

Ben gave Usha a stern look.

"Just do it Ben" Usha shouted.

"Okay, Okay", Ben replied, "Anything to keep the peace.

Usha kissed Ben on the cheek. "Trust me" Usha said.

Usha got her phone out and quickly phoned for an ambulance to attend Mrs Beans' house where Chloe was staying. Within two minutes, the sound of a siren could be heard as the ambulance sped up the hill.

"We'd better get off to our lessons Ben" Usha said.

"S'pose" Ben muttered. "I'll catch up with you later", he added.

Richard drove his van onto the drive at Lillys' house. His Granddaughter was sat outside on one of the benches.

"Hi Grandad" Lilly said.

"Hi princess" Richard replied and kissed her on the cheek. "How's things?" Richard asked.

"Well ...." Lilly hesitated and then she told him how herself and Usha had communicated and been in Chloes' dream. And hopefully, how they'd saved Chloes' life.

"Wow" exclaimed Richard. "And I thought I was having a bad day" he added.

"Someone at the hospital isn't doing their job right and I think I know who it is. There should have been a toxicology report done on Chloes' Mum. If there had have been, Chloe might not be where she is now." Richard continued.

"How do you feel now Lilly?" Richard asked.

"Yeah, I'm okay. I'm just so worried about Chloe" Lilly replied.

"I thought I saw the ambulance travelling at speed up to Mrs Beans' house. Hopefully, they got to Chloe in time" Richard said.

"It's not just that though Grandad. Chloe knows. She definitely knows about us" Lilly replied with an anxious tone in her voice.

Lilly continued, "I don't know how she knows, but I saw it in her sub conscious today. Chloe knows about the amulet and the Treasure Of Lima. I also saw a vague memory of a map, a really old map. There was just so much going on in her head, it was difficult to unravel all the information"

"We knew there was a chance that something like this could happen when we made the decision to clear the blood clot in her brain at the hospital Lilly" Richard replied. "The point is, how do we get round the problem?" Richard asked.

Lilly shrugged her shoulders, "I don't have any ideas at the moment" Lilly said, "This particular power of mind control is obviously a two way thing, don't you think?" Lilly asked.

Lilly continued "The other thing to consider is the fact that Chloe sub consciously must have got into my head whilst I was asleep. She contacted me. Probably a cry for help".

"Hmmm ... well at least we've got a couple of days to think it through," Richard answered, "but the priority for now is Chloes' well being eh?"

"You're right" Lilly said.

Lilly glanced at her watch. "Sorry Grandad, I need to go. I'm looking after the café this afternoon". Lilly gave Richard a kiss on the cheek and a hug. "I'll see you later perhaps", and with a wave, she disappeared on her scooter.

What the hell are we going to do? Richard thought as he climbed back in his van. *What if ....* "Run to the Hills" by Iron Maiden was playing on his phone. It was his ring tone. *Who's this?* he thought as he answered.

"Is that Richard?" a voice in his ear. It was Beth, the nurse at the hospital.

"Hi Beth, what's up?" Richard asked.

"We've a problem with Chloe and my lad Alex, seems to think you can help" Beth said.

"Ask away" Richard replied.

Beth explained, "Chloe's taken an overdose. Obviously we're pumping her stomach out, but there's a problem. We don't know what she's taken and we can't treat her in case there's a reaction".

"You must have the bottle" Richard said.

"What bottle Richard?"

There was a moments pause as Richard fought with his conscience.

"You're going to have to trust me on this Beth" Richard replied, and then continued, "She had a bottle of tablets that were her Mums. They were given to Mrs Mollins by Dr Perez".

"That explains a lot Richard" Beth replied. "The doctor was on the ambulance that attended to Chloe earlier. He must have removed the bottle to cover his tracks" Beth added.

"That sounds about right" Richard replied and then continued "But he's not stupid. He'll have got rid of the bottle by now. Beth, you need to ring the Medical Centre and urgently request Mrs Mollins' medical records. They'll give you the answer you're looking for".

"Thanks Richard, I'll get on it" Beth replied.

"No probs Beth …. and please, no questions asked" Richard said.

"Richard, I trust you, believe me" Beth said and then disconnected.

School was finished for the day. Ben and Usha were sat on one of the benches outside, waiting for Luis and Lilly to pick them up on their scooters. Ben and his girlfriend were discussing the day at school and how it had seemed rather boring, apart that is from Ushas' 'episode'.

Luis turned up first to Ushas' disgust.

The three friends were laughing and joking when the distinctive sound of Lillys' four stroke scooter could be heard approaching.

"That's Lilly" the three teenagers shouted in unison, and they started to laugh.

Luis watched intently as Lilly drove up the school drive, her blond hair blowing in the wind. He could immediately smell her perfume in the air as she stopped the scooters' engine in front of them. She gave a big smile as she dismounted the vehicle.

"Hi guys" Lilly said. "How we all doing?" she asked.

"You're late" Usha muttered.

"Sorry sis', couldn't be helped. Been busy at the café this afternoon", Lilly explained. She turned and kissed Luis on the lips.

That's rather nice, Luis thought.

"How's Chloe?" Usha asked and continued, "Does anyone know?"

"I caught up with Alex earlier" Luis said. "He was a bit shook up actually" Luis added.

"Apparently he'd been fixing his scooter outside his house and he thought Chloe was asleep in bed. He got a phone call from young Ben here, telling him to check on Chloe. When he did, he found Chloe unconscious, apparently from an overdose of drugs and then the ambulance turned up just in time. Alex is up at the hospital now with Chloe" Luis explained and then added, "So Ben's the hero of the day."

Lilly and Usha gave each other a knowing look and smiled.

CHAPTER 17

It was the weekend and the island had seemingly become busy overnight due to a Dark Skies Festival. The hotels, along with various self catering and bed and breakfast establishments were bursting at the seams. Even the camp site at Saye Bay had seen an increase in numbers. The last time Alderney had seen visitor numbers like this was back in August 1999 when the island experienced a total solar eclipse.

Alderney is unique in that there is little or no artificial light pollution at night. Astronomy has seen a boom over the years and star gazers will travel anywhere to gain access to dark clear skies to record and photograph phenomenon of great interest.

There was an added bonus this particular weekend for the younger generation. Bunker Parties!

The Alderney Bunker Parties are legendary for anyone that visits on a regular basis. These parties take place in any one of the old World War II German Bunkers underground and are all night affairs until five or six in the morning. Some of these are huge complexs' and have been wired up with lighting and sound systems ready for all night raves and discos for all ages. And there's always plenty of booze flowing.

This weekend is going to be awesome, Usha thought.

Lilly and Luis were meeting up with Usha and their friends in about an hour outside the Braye Chippy. In the meantime they had a bit of catching up to do. They were at Lillys'.

Her Mum and Dad were out joining in on a night time walk with some of their friends up to the Butes Cricket Ground where a BBQ was being held.

Luis walked up the stairs and reached the landing, glancing around for Lillys' bedroom.

"Where are you Lilly?" Luis asked.

"Second room on your left" Lilly replied. She smiled to herself as she looked at herself in the full length mirror. She could feel the hairs on the back of her neck bristling with anticipation.

Luis stood in the open doorway. He glanced in and he felt his heart racing as he looked adoringly at the girl he'd fallen in love with. Lilly stood perfectly still, wearing just the smallest of panties to cover her modesty. As she watched in the mirror, Luis' eyes were wandering, *and probably lusting over my body,* she thought.

Lillys' body is so perfect in every way, Luis thought. She was slim with an hour glass figure. She turned to face Luis, and as she raised her arms, her hands clasped her long blond hair to reveal soft pert breasts with nipples straining to be caressed.

Luis could feel his emotions almost jumping for joy uncontrollably ....

"Luis... Luis!" Lillys' voice reverberated down the stairs.

Luis shook himself. He'd been day dreaming whilst he'd been looking at a framed photo of Lilly on the table. *Jeez,* he thought.

"Luis" Lilly shouted. "Are you there?"

"Err... yeah, coming" Luis replied.

As he climbed the stairs, Lilly shouted again. "Second room on the left".

"I know" Luis replied. *No, surely not,* he thought to himself.

He stood in the open doorway to see Lilly stood in front of her full length mirror with her back to Luis. *This is really feeling weird,* Luis thought.

"Don't just stand there gawping" Lilly said. "Zip the back of my dress up please".

Luis walked into her bedroom. He gently pulled the zip up and then kissed the back of Lillys' neck.

Lilly spun round and took a step back from Luis.

"Well?.... What d'you think?" Lilly asked.

"Perfect …. Absolutely stunning" Luis replied.

Lilly spun round again. She was wearing a slightly tarty number. A red mini dress with a Chinese style pattern that sat tightly around her thighs. A low cut plunging neckline that left little to the imagination as her pert fulsome breasts strained to contain themselves.

"Wow" Luis exclaimed. "I'm gonna have to keep an eye on you at the party".

Lilly leant forward and threw her arms around Luis' neck and kissed him passionately on the lips.

"Don't worry, I'm all yours" Lilly replied.

"Come on gal, let's get going" Luis said.

Luis clambered onto his scooter. "What are you waiting for?" he asked Lilly. He had a big grin on his face. "How are you going to get on in that dress?"

"Watch me" Lilly responded. She held the lower part of her dress and shuffled it up over her upper thighs to reveal her panties. Lilly threw her one leg over the pillion seat and she was on.

"You sure about this?" Luis asked.

"Absolutely" Lilly said. "They're clean" she joked.

"Okay … just hang on tightly" Luis shouted as he revved the engine and pulled away.

Minutes later, they arrived at Braye Chippy. *There must be over three hundred people down here,* Lilly thought.

Luis was off his scooter first and immediately was aware of the whistles and woo wooing from the lads in the huge crowd.

Lilly held Luis' hand and slid off the machine. She waved to the crowd with unadulterated bliss and blew them kisses to an even greater cheer of approval.

"Lilly, you're embarrassing me" Luis muttered.

"Come on, lighten up, it's just a bit of fun" Lilly replied as she encouraged her dress down her thighs. She bowed to the crowd and laughed.

"Thought it might be you putting on a show" Usha said. "You're a hussy" she joked.

Usha and Ben had been filling their faces with snacks and bacon butties whilst they'd been waiting. "There's a BBQ just round the corner at the Moorings" Ben said. "We've been listening to one of the live bands playing. They're great".

The Moorings is a restaurant come bar with a decked area looking out over Braye Bay and regularly host live bands and artists.

As the four friends listened they could hear the thumping guitar track of Radar Love by Golden Earring resonating through the sea air.

"Love this track" Luis said, "One of my faves".

A group of lads strolled by giving Lilly the once over. "Hi Lilly, looking good gal" they shouted.

"Thanks guys" Lilly replied and she gave them a pose.

Luis stood there glaring.

"Here comes another scooter guys" Usha shouted. "There must be at least fifty down here now".

"It's Alex, he must have fixed his scooter" Lilly said as she pointed down the road. "He's got Chloe with him... Cool".

"Hi guys" Alex shouted as he switched the engine off. "Look at all these people".

Chloe got off the scooter. Ben, Usha and Luis each hugged and kissed her in turn.

"Look at you girl" Lilly said as she put her arms around Chloe and held her tight. "Good to see you out and about. And you look so much better".

"I'm good thanks" Chloe replied, "Just look at you gal, quite the glamour girl this evening…. and look at the lads round here, they're all giving you the come on". And the two girls laughed and kissed each other.

A music track by the band Garbage drifted through the air and it seemed as if the hundreds of teenagers present were singing in unison as they jumped and danced around…"Don't believe in fear, Don't believe in faith, Don't believe in anything That you can't break. You stupid girl, You stupid girl, All you had you wasted, All you had you wasted".

"This is just brill" Alex shouted "Just what Chloe needs, a bit of girl bonding".

"And a drop of booze" Chloe added with a smile.

"Oh yes … Awesome" Usha shouted.

"I'll get the drinks in then" Luis said. "Anyone want to help me?"

"Come on Luis, I'll help" Ben replied, "Won't be long guys". And the two lads disappeared into the crowd to find the bar.

"Well that leaves me with three pretty girls" Alex said jokingly as he stood with his arm around Chloes' waist. She kissed him on the cheek.

"So, how are we getting to the bunker party?" Usha asked, "'Cos it's a long walk, which sucks".

"Grandad's going to pick us up and take us all" Lilly replied, "In about ten minutes" as she glanced at her watch. "Hmmm, the boys will have to be quick with the drinks".

"Did you behave yourself earlier?" Usha asked with that impish grin on her face, "When you was by yourself with Luis".

"Of course I did" Lilly snapped back, and then with a really naughty look, she added "But I did tease him".

The four friends laughed, with Usha and Chloe waving a single finger side to side in Lillys' face.

Ben and Luis had struggled to get to the bar and decided on six bottles of beer. *No spillage on the way back,* Ben thought. As they pushed and shoved their way back through the crowd they came to a stop. Luis turned to Ben, "Do you think Lilly's a tease?" Luis asked.

"No I wouldn't say that mate" Ben replied. "But she's very mature for her age and she knows what she wants …why?"

"It's probably nothing", Luis answered, "But there's been the odd occasion like earlier today where I didn't feel in control of the situation. It was if she was giving me the come on, and not for the first time".

"Ha … lucky you" Ben said, "Come on, we need to get back to the others before Lilly pulls some other guy". Ben gave Luis a wink.

The hard rock pounding of The Scorpions grew louder as the two lads pushed their way through the crowd.

"Someone's got a good taste in music" Luis said "Another one of my faves, it's called The Zoo".

"I meet my girl, She's dressed to kill, And all we gonna do Is walk around to catch the thrill". *Brilliant* thought Luis.

Finally the two lads reached their friends who were dancing and singing to the music. They all gathered round for their beers.

"Cheers" Lilly shouted as she thrust her arm to the evening sky. The friends cheered and clinked their bottles.

"Anyone for another?" Ben shouted over the thumping music.

Lilly bent her head towards Bens' ear, "My Grandad will be here in a minute to pick us up and take all of us up to the Bunker Party".

"What about our scooters?" Ben asked.

"When my Grandad's dropped us off he's going to come back here and pick them up" Lilly explained, "And he'll take the scooters to our houses".

"Cool" Ben replied.

Richard carefully drove his van through the crowds that were encroaching onto the road as he approached the Braye Chippy. *Jeez, haven't seen this number of people down here in years,* Richard thought.

"Come on guys" Richard shouted to himself, "Get out of the way".

He could see Lilly and her friends about fifty metres away and he started to honk the horn on the van to draw their attention. *Looks like they're already having a good time,* Richard thought.

The van pulled up and Richard climbed out. The sound of music was deafening and Richard waved to a few familiar faces in the crowd. He was well known on the island.

The young friends ambled over to Richard.

"Hi guys" Richard said, struggling to make his voice heard.

"Hi Mr Morgan", the friends shouted.

"Hi Grandad" Lilly said as she kissed him on the cheek.

"Look at you young lady....all grown up" Richard said, "A bit tarty don't you think?" he said with an evil glint in his eyes and a big grin.

"Come on guys, let's get going" Usha shouted.

They all clambered into the van accompanied by cheers and shouts from the crowd as Lilly struggled to contain her body in the tight dress.

Jeez, thought Richard, *we're gonna have to keep an eye on you girl.* He smiled to himself.

As Richard drove along the coast road he glanced in his rear view mirror. The teenagers were all preoccupied kissing each other and laughing and joking. *The good old days,* Richard thought to himself.

"Hold on" Richard shouted as the van hit the tight bend at the bottom of Tourgis Hill. He laughed to himself as the teenagers rolled across the floor of the van in fits of giggles.

Richard drove past Fort Tourgis on his right, and onwards to the junction near the airport. He steered the van onto the grass track which would take them to the Bunker Party. It was a bumpy ride in which the teenagers shouted or cheered at every bump. The track continued through overgrown vegetation until a large flat open space opened up in front of them and Richard pulled the van over to a stop.

This was the Giffaine in the south west of the island. It was aptly named The Guns by the local population because this vast expanse of land was littered with German World War II fortifications, some above ground and many below. Huge concrete structures with walls two metres thick in places. Many of the gun emplacements and bunkers have been hidden for decades by brambles and wild vegetation, whilst others have been cleared for tourism and in this case, a Bunker Party.

For the uninitiated, the whole area feels surreal and creepy. At night, it's in total darkness, you have to be brave, or mad, or both!

Tonight, lights were shining at strategic points powered by a diesel generator. Crowds were milling around, drinking and waiting for friends. Rave music could be heard emanating from below ground. All rather surreal... but exciting.

"Okay guys, everyone out" Richard said as he slid the side door open.

"Awesome" Usha shouted.

"Thanks for the lift Mr Morgan" Chloe said.

"Right guys, you got everything?" Richard asked. "Phones, torches, money?"

Lilly and Usha hugged Richard. "Don't worry Grandad, we'll be fine" Lilly assured him.

"Hmmm, we'll see. Take care of each other" Richard replied. He turned to the others, "Enjoy yourselves guys".

Richard climbed back in his van and drove out into the darkness. *Pick up the scooters,* he thought.

"Right guys, this is my treat" Alex announced and he pulled out six coloured wrist bands, one for each of them. "You need to wear these to gain access to the Bunker Party".

Chloe flung her arms around Alex and kissed him. "They must have cost you a fair bit of money" she said.

Alex shrugged his shoulders, "You'll just have to help me find more golf balls" he joked.

"Thanks Alex" his friends shouted.

"Right, let's do it" Lilly shouted and grabbed Luis' hand.

The entrance to the bunker complex was three metres below ground level accessed by a grassy sloping path.

"Careful as you walk down here" Luis said, "It's a bit slippy".

"You got that right" Usha replied. She carefully negotiated the slope holding Bens' hand as they walked behind Lilly and Luis. Chloe and Alex were close behind.

At the bottom of the slope the friends turned to their left and entered the gloomy, dimly lit corridor and as they walked further, the beating sound of techno music became louder with every step.

They turned another corner and were met by a couple of familiar faces, two local lads that organised the Bunker Parties every year. Tim and Adam were checking all entrants for their wrist bands and drugs.

"Hi guys, long time no see" Adam said, "If you don't mind guys, we just need to check you over. You know how it is these days".

"Yeah sure" Lilly replied "There you go" and she stretched her arms out to each side at shoulder height, forcing her dress to ride up high on her thighs and her bosom to heave to bursting point.

"Err yeah, thanks Lilly" Adam said. He could feel his face glowing.

"Don't think you'll find anything in there mate" Tim joked.

"Sorry Adam" Lilly said, "Couldn't resist it" and they all burst out laughing.

"Go in guys, get out of here" Adam joked with a knowing look to Lilly.

The friends walked further down the corridor in high spirits. A huge concrete room opened before them filled with old friends and visitors. The place was heaving shoulder to shoulder and the music was pounding out its' rhythm from the next room. Some bunkers have up to twenty rooms depending on the size of the concrete structure.

"Where's the bar?" Chloe asked.

"Over there" Ben replied. He pointed to one of the rooms over to the left.

"Right, let's start as we mean to go on" Alex said. The friends eased themselves through the dancers into the next room and grabbed a few bottles of beer.

"The music's great" Usha shouted.

"Come on, let's go to that room over there where the main action is" Lilly said, and she grabbed Luis by the arm and led him into the main room followed by their friends.

The DJ's were busy with playing the various tracks of music. The lighting system was working a treat as different coloured pulsing rays of light were dancing around the room.

Throbbing lights were everywhere creating strange patterns on the concrete walls. The music continued endlessly into the early hours of the morning. Lilly and her friends danced and sang as the night passed by. Empty bottles of beer were stacking up as the teenagers became more uninhibited as the booze took hold.

As the hours went by the number of party revellers had dwindled, but somehow the friends had become separated. The music pounded on.

I need some air, Lilly thought. She gradually pushed her way through the dancers until she was outside at the bottom of the slope. The cold air hit her like a sledgehammer. Her head was spinning but she managed to stagger up the slope.

She sat down briefly on one of the many plastic chairs dotted around and noticed other teenagers sitting and lying around as they chatted amongst themselves. Lilly glanced up at the stars in the clear sky. *That's the Orion constellation there,* Lilly thought.

"Hi Lilly" a voice from behind made her jump. It was Usha.

"Have you seen the others?" Usha asked.

"Not for some time sis'" Lilly replied.

"Lilly…. My pendant has started pulsing" Usha exclaimed, "And look, your amulet is as well".

Lilly jumped up with a look of trepidation on her face.

"Lilly, what's going on?" Usha muttered.

"Usha, what's up?" Lilly asked. "Usha, talk to me".

Usha was transfixed. Her pendant was pulsing steadily and then her eyes turned red.

"Usha …. What the…" Lilly stuttered as Usha started to walk slowly away as if controlled by some external force.

Lilly quickly pulled a torch out of Ushas' pocket and turned it on so she could follow her sister. Usha continued to walk until another underground bunker complex came into view.

Lilly watched intently as Usha made her way down some steps to the entrance which was blocked by a large rusty wrought iron gate. It was padlocked.

Lilly stood next to Usha and shone the torch down the corridor. It looked very much like the Party Bunker they'd left. Usha suddenly heaved a big sigh.

"Sis', you okay?" Lilly asked.

"Why are we here?" Usha replied.

Lilly shrugged her shoulders "Don't know. But there's obviously a reason. Your pendant and my amulet are still pulsing as well. I think we need to get in here. Your pendant brought us here so we need to take a look".

"Agreed" Usha replied. "But how?" She pointed to the padlock.

"No probs" Lilly said and threw her hand forward. The padlock dropped to the ground. "Give us a hand to open this gate 'cos it's rusted up and heavy. The two girls pulled the gate open as it creaked and groaned.

"Come on Usha" Lilly said, "Let's take a look. Just be careful where you walk. We need to stay close".

The girls gingerly walked down the corridor. The torch light was creating all manner of weird looking shapes as Lilly shone the light back and forth until they reached the main room. Other corridors and rooms were visible, identical to the Party Bunker. They stood in the centre of the circular room.

"Lilly, look up there" Usha said as she pointed upwards. "You can see the stars".

There was a two metre diameter circular hole in the roof.

"Probably where the gun mounting used to be" Lilly said.

Lilly stood directly beneath the hole and realised it framed the Orion Constellation in the sky above. Her amulet started to pulse stronger and brighter. She felt in control. Lilly stepped aside and beckoned Usha to stand exactly where she had just stood.

"Tell me what you see sis'" Lilly said.

"The Orion Constellation" Usha replied "And?"

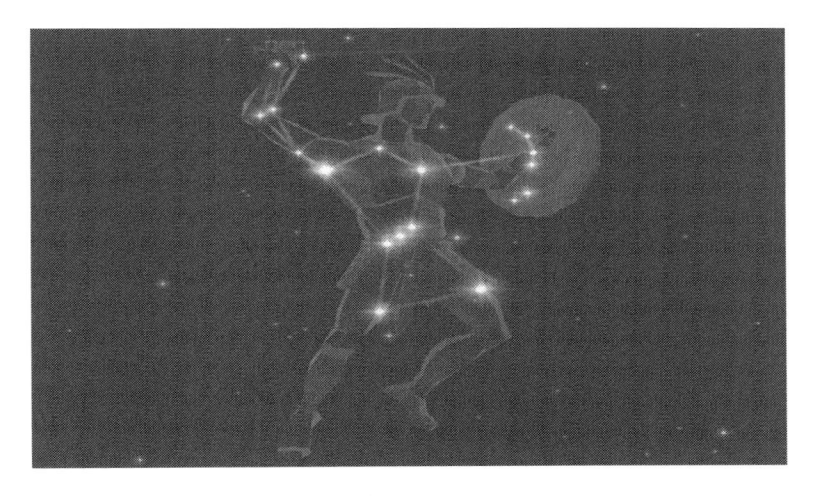

"Look at your pendant" Lilly replied.

Ushas' pendant was pulsing brighter and stronger.

"Don't touch it until we know what's happening" Lilly said.

"Do as Lilly says Usha", a voice from behind the girls. It was Chloe and stood with her was Richard who had his hand on Chloes' shoulder.

"Chloe, Grandad, what are you doing here?" Lilly asked with an astonished look on her face.

Usha stood open mouthed in disbelief.

Chloe reached around her neck and revealed a dark red pendant on a gold chain.

"That's exactly the same as mine" Usha exclaimed "And it's pulsing in exactly the same rhythm as mine".

"Not only that" Richard said as he pulled his sleeve up "My amulet is doing exactly the same thing".

"Awesome" Usha cried out.

"Chloe....How?....Why didn't you tell us? Lilly asked with a distinct frustrated voice.

"Sorry Lilly .... Long story for later" Chloe replied.

"We were all 'summoned' here for some reason" Richard said.

Chloe had stepped to the centre of the room and stood under the gaping hole in the concrete above. She looked up to gaze at the Orion Constellation and immediately grabbed hold of her pulsing pendant hanging around her neck.

"No don't" Richard shouted.

Too late. Chloe stood there in a trance like state, her eyes glowing dark red. "I am a child of the stars" she cried out loudly.

"Stay back girls" Richard shouted, "This is really weird stuff".

Chloe held out her arms to the side and instantly a beam of light concentrated on her pendant. Richard looked up to see the beam was coming from the middle star, Alnitak, that forms part of Orions' Belt.

"Girls, grab my hands and hold Chloes' hands to form a circle. I've an idea" Richard shouted.

The foursome stood in a circle joined by their hands and suddenly three further beams of light passed through the hole above and concentrated on Ushas' pendant and the two amulets of Richard and Lilly. Two beams were emanating from the other stars in Orions' Belt, Alnilam, and Mintaka. The third beam was from the star in Orions' Sword and was concentrating on Richards' amulet. The four of them were completely helpless until suddenly the beams of light disappeared. They all collapsed in a heap.

Moments later, the three girls and Richard stirred. "Everyone okay?" Richard asked with a concerned look on his face as the girls slowly got themselves to their feet. They glanced at each other in bemusement.

Usha pointed at Chloe, "Your hair Chloe, look at your hair. It's …. it's".

"We know Usha, it's awesome" Lilly interrupted.

Usha giggled.

Chloe pulled her long black hair around her shoulders, "I've got a blonde streak. What the …".

"Very becoming young lady" Richard said, and he smiled at her.

"So, I'm confused here" Lilly said, "What just happened here and what is Chloe doing here?"

"Yeah, come on Grandad, what IS Chloe doing here?" Usha shouted impatiently.

Richard gave Chloe a knowing glance.

"First things first" Richard said "Has anyone got any recollection of what just happened?… 'cos strangely I have a picture of part of a map in my head".

"So have I" Chloe said.

"And we have too" Lilly and Usha added.

"Hmmm, okay then. It's far too late to do anything now" Richard said as he glanced at his watch showing four thirty in the morning. "We need to get out of here and back to the boys".

"But what about Chloe?" Usha asked.

"Look" Richard said "We'll get together this afternoon. Me and Chloe will explain everything…. Now then, we need to go guys".

"Sort the padlock out Lilly on the way out" Richard said.

Richard and the girls climbed the steps back onto the grass track. It was just before dawn and there was a fresh westerly wind blowing in off the sea.

"Let's find the lads" Richard said as he led the way back to the Party Bunker. "It looks like a battlefield here" he joked.

Empty bottles, crates and left over food was scattered over a large area. A good forty or so party goers were either sitting around suffering with hangovers or sleeping the booze off.

"There they are" Chloe shouted "Talk about sleeping like babies" she joked.

"I'll leave you to it then" Richard said as he climbed in his van. "I take it you lot are walking?"

The girls nodded and smiled.

"We'll meet this afternoon yeah, I'll text you later", Richard waved and drove off.

CHAPTER 18

It's a lovely afternoon, Richard thought, as he planted up the last tomato plant in the greenhouse. The sun was beating down, the many birds in the garden were singing. *This is bliss,* he thought. *A bit of me time before the girls arrive.* He hadn't really given it much thought since he left them earlier that day, but now it was dawning on him that today would be important in so many ways. Possibly life changing.

"Run to the Hills", Richards' ring tone interrupted his thoughts.

"Hi Richard, it's Beth. Sorry to bother you today. You okay".

"Oh hi Beth" Richard answered, "Yeah I'm fine thanks. What's up?"

"I thought you might like to know that Dr Perez has left the island" Beth replied.

"Why does that not surprise me. So does anyone know where he's gone?" Richard asked.

"Not yet. All they do know is that he left the island last night on a chartered boat heading for France" Beth explained "He took advantage of all the celebrations around the island hoping that no-one would notice".

"So I take it the Police were on to him?" Richard asked.

"Oh yeah, for sure" Beth replied, "Since the incident with Chloe they've been digging around".

"I'm sure they'll realise what's been going on" Richard said "And they'll be more revelations to shock everyone. I'm sure of that Beth".

"Well, the Police did tell me that Interpol had been notified" Beth said "So it sounds like it's seriously heavy stuff".

" Karma springs to mind" Richard replied, "Does young Chloe know about this?"

"I believe so … why?" Beth asked.

"Nothing really. It's just that Chloe and my girls are coming up to see me and they're due any minute" Richard replied. He glanced at his watch.

"Well Richard, I'd better let you go. I just thought you would like to know" Beth said "And by the way, thanks for the info the other day".

"No probs Beth. You take care". Richard hung up.

"Hi Grandad" Usha called out as she walked into the back garden followed by Lilly and Chloe. The three girls took it turn to kiss Richard on the cheek.

"This is all very nice" Richard joked, "We should do this more often. Let's sit down shall we".

They all sat under the willow tree to take advantage of the dappled shade it provided from the hot afternoon sun. The three girls all looked at Richard in anticipation of what was to come.

"Where shall I start?" Richard asked himself. He looked towards Chloe and she nodded reassuringly.

"I've spoken to your Grandma about this and she is of the same opinion that the three of you need to know something that's really important" Richard said in a serious tone of voice. "You see …. the three of you are related". There was a long silence, then …..

"What. What do you mean Grandad?" Usha stuttered. "How CAN we be related?" she asked.

"Let me explain please and then you can ask as many questions as you like. Okay?"

The three girls nodded.

Richard went on to explain that he once had a son called Philip, that Lilly and Usha had never met. Many years ago, Philip had a big fall out with the family and he never spoke to them again. In fact, he went so far as changing his surname by deed poll from Morgan to Mollins.

Lilly glanced at Chloe. Her eyes were welling up with tears.

"He was my Dad" Chloe blurted out and sobbed.

"Oh Chloe" Lilly said in a caring voice.

Usha placed her arm around Chloes' shoulders to try and comfort her friend …. her cousin …. "You're our cousin" Usha shouted. "How long have you known about this?"

"I've always known, but my Dad wouldn't let me talk about it. He'd even threaten me sometimes" Chloe said. "It was the same with my Mum".

"And I couldn't tell anyone 'cos it would have caused more trouble with Philip" Richard added.

"Did you ever make up with Uncle Philip, Grandad?" Lilly asked.

"Yeah sure, about a year before he died" Richard replied "But by then, Chloes' family life was set in stone, so to speak".

Richard went on to explain further, his best friend Dave Haynes who used to own the workshop below Fort Tourgis, also rented the bunker up on the Guns where they'd all experienced the Orion phenomenon. The bunkers in disrepair on Alderney are rented out for private use and Dave used to grow mushrooms in that bunker because the conditions were ideal.

"Dave found the pendant that Chloe now has, in that very bunker and that's why I think it drew us all there", Richard said. "I used to go up to the bunker with Dave to help him with his mushrooms and he showed me the pendant he'd found. For whatever reason, Dave was adamant that he would give it to Philip when the time was right".

Richard continued to explain that Dave gave Philip the pendant just before he died. And about six weeks later, Philip died in a car accident and Chloe was in the car as well.

"I was in the back seat and suddenly the steering failed on the car, but Dad had no chance to stop the car". Chloe blurted out. She was sobbing uncontrollably. "The car ran into the back of a bus. The last thing I remember was, as my Dad was taking his last breaths he gave me the pendant and told me not to wear it unless my life was in danger".

Richard held Chloes' hand to try and comfort her. He then went on to explain that Chloes' Mum, Carol, had been having an affair with Dr Perez unbeknown to Philip.

"I thought at the time and still do that Dr Perez was responsible for both Daves' and Philips' deaths" Richard explained, "They both knew along with me, that Dr Perezs' Grandparents had lived in Peru. The doctor was born there and it's likely that he had corrupt connections in South America. We all thought that Dr Perez knew about the existence of the Lima Treasure and therefore he would use any means to get his hands on it".

Richard went on to explain that his son Philip was investigating Dr Perez at the time of his death. Philip had told Richard that Dave had died of an overdose and his doctor was Perez.

"The next thing I heard was that Philip had died in a car crash whilst in the UK and that the Police were treating it as suspicious" Richard said, "They knew that the steering had been tampered with but had no clues as to when and where. I later found out from Carol, that Dr Perez had borrowed the car for a couple of days before it was transported to the UK".

"So you think that Dr Perez was after Chloes' pendant and the Lima Treasure?" Lilly asked.

"Oh for sure" Richard replied. He then told the girls about his earlier conversation on the phone with Beth, the nurse.

"So he's done a runner then" Usha added.

"Dr Perez has also left other casualties behind eh Chloe?" Richard said as he glanced at his recently revealed Granddaughter.

Chloe nodded in agreement.

"As I said, Dr Perez was having an affair with Chloes' Mum, Carol, with the auterior motive of finding Philips' pendant" Richard explained, "Carol had a growing drink problem since the death of Philip and she didn't realise that Dr Perez was spiking her drinks with a cocktail of drugs, which explained her mood swings. The doctor would prescribe her all manner of pills in an attempt to coheres her into revealing the location of the pendant".

"What a jerk" Usha shouted.

"It's terrible how desperate people get" Lilly added.

Richard went on, "Dr Perez then saw his chance with Chloe, after the incident at home with her Mum. He was there at the hospital and again, he was there at Alexs' house when Chloe was staying over. He knew that Chloe had her Mums' tablets and he was going to take advantage of the situation".

"Yeah, he knew alright" Chloe interrupted. "But this time, I was one step ahead of him. I knew it was going to be dangerous but I had to trust my instinct, that between them, Lilly and Usha would save my life".

"Wow" exclaimed Usha.

Chloe explained "After I'd spent the night at Alexs', the following morning I stayed in bed whilst Alex was outside fixing his scooter. His Mum had already gone to work. At some point I had to go to the bathroom and through a side window I saw Dr Perezs' car outside. I shouted out for Alex but I think he must have given himself a break and wandered off".

"So what did you do?" Lilly asked.

"Well I realised that this was the moment" Chloe replied, and continued "I rushed back to the bedroom and grabbed the pendant out of my bag and shoved it down the side of my ankle sock. I heard the sound of footsteps coming up the stairs and then ... Dr Perez entered the bedroom. He was cussing in some sort of foreign language and I could see the fury in his eyes as he grabbed my wrists". Chloe held her wrists out to show them the scars. "He then forced me down onto the bed. I kicked out but he was too heavy and strong for me and then ...."

"What?" Usha asked impatiently.

"He stuck a needle in my arm, a hypo" Chloe said, "Some sort of sedative I think. All I remember is him forcing a bottle of tablets down my throat and ...

"And that's when you connected with me" Usha interrupted.

"Wow" Lilly said. "That's some serious grief".

The group were interrupted by steps from behind and a voice, "Who wants a drink?" It was Bea, Richards' wife. She placed the tray of drinks on the table.

"Thanks Hun'" Richard said as he smiled approvingly.

"So I gather you've told the girls then Richard?" Bea asked.

"Of course" he replied.

"So girls, what d'ya think?" Bea asked.

"It's ...." Usha hesitated.

"Awesome" the three girls shouted as they ran to their Grandma and gave her a hug.

Bea placed her hands on Lillys' head, then Ushas' and finally Chloe, "Love the blonde streak" she joked.

Chloe hugged Bea once more, "I love you Grandma".

"It's lovely to hear you say that... Finally after all this time we're a proper family again" Bea said with tears welling up in her eyes.

"We all love you Grandma" Lilly shouted as they each gave Bea another hug and kiss.

"The Three Marys back together again" Bea said.

"What did you say Grandma?" Lilly asked.

"The Three Marys" replied Bea, "The three of you all have a second name. It's Mary. You were all given that name after your Great Grandmothers' name, Mary Morgan".

Richard nodded in agreement.

"Of course, that's it" Lilly exclaimed. "The Latin Americans call the three stars in Orions' Belt, The Three Marys". Lilly gave Usha and Chloe a knowing look.

Bea interrupted, "I haven't a clue what you're on about young lady. But it sounds interesting anyway".

ALDERNEY

Look out for the next book in the series

VISITORS

Printed by Amazon Italia Logistica S.r.l.
Torrazza Piemonte (TO), Italy